THE
INSIDE JOB

(And Other Skills I Learned as a Superspy)

Also by Jackson Pearce

The Doublecross (And Other Skills I Learned as a Superspy)

THE INSIDE

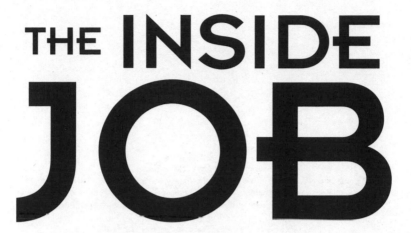

JOB

AND OTHER SKILLS
I LEARNED AS A
SUPERSPY

JACKSON PEARCE

BLOOMSBURY

NEW YORK LONDON OXFORD NEW DELHI SYDNEY

First published in the United States of America in July 2016
by Bloomsbury Children's Books
www.bloomsbury.com

Bloomsbury is a registered trademark of Bloomsbury Publishing Plc

For information about permission to reproduce selections from this book, write to
Permissions, Bloomsbury Children's Books, 1385 Broadway, New York, New York 10018
Bloomsbury books may be purchased for business or promotional use. For information on bulk purchases
please contact Macmillan Corporate and Premium Sales Department at specialmarkets@macmillan.com

Library of Congress Cataloging-in-Publication Data
Names: Pearce, Jackson, author.
Title: The inside job : (and other skills I learned as a superspy) /
by Jackson Pearce.
Description: New York : Bloomsbury Childrens Books, 2016. | Sequel to: Doublecross.
Summary: Together with his friends, twelve-year-old Hale, an overweight and non-athletic double agent
against SRS, the corrupt spy organization he was raised in, travels to Switzerland to destroy the SRS
bank account.
Identifiers: LCCN 2015025273
ISBN 978-1-61963-420-6 (hardcover) • ISBN 978-1-61963-421-3 (e-book)
Subjects: | CYAC: Spies—Fiction. | Adventure and adventurers—Fiction. | Friendship—Fiction. |
Overweight persons—Fiction. | Ability—Fiction. | Switzerland—Fiction. | BISAC: JUVENILE FICTION/
Action & Adventure/General. | JUVENILE FICTION/Humorous Stories. | JUVENILE FICTION/Social
Issues/Friendship.
Classification: LCC PZ7.P31482 In 2016 | DDC [Fic]—dc23
LC record available at http://lccn.loc.gov/2015025273

Book design by Yelena Safronova and Nicole Gastonguay
Typeset by Newgen Knowledge Works (P) Ltd., Chennai, India
Printed and bound in the U.S.A. by Berryville Graphics Inc., Berryville, Virginia
2 4 6 8 10 9 7 5 3 1

All papers used by Bloomsbury Publishing, Inc., are natural, recyclable products
made from wood grown in well-managed forests. The manufacturing processes
conform to the environmental regulations of the country of origin.

For Mom,
who likes Hale best

THE
INSIDE JOB

(And Other Skills I Learned as a Superspy)

CHAPTER ONE

I'm a spy.

I speak eight languages fluently and am conversational in another three. I can rewire a car and disarm most explosives. I've been building up my tolerance to poisons since I was four years old, and I can pick a lock in less than a minute and break into a safe in less than three—usually. (The giant safes take a little longer, obviously.) I've spent my entire life studying, training, and practicing to be the best spy I can possibly be.

And yet, I was about to be chucked over a fence.

Mission: Break into a highly secured building
Step 1: Make it through the exterior fence

It was at least seven feet tall, with another few feet of barbed wire across the top. My little sister, Kennedy, was able to spring up the fence and slip under the barbed wire like some sort of redheaded lemur. But Walter, my best friend, was too big to fit between the barbed wire and the fence. So, his plan was to climb the side of a nearby delivery truck, jump from there over the fence, latch on to a drainpipe, and then leap from the drainpipe to the ground.

It was a pretty athletic plan. But Walter was a pretty athletic guy.

"What about you?" Walter asked as he bounded from the ground to the hood of the truck in one swift movement.

"Let me think," I said. Like Walter, I couldn't fit between the barbed wire and the fence. Unlike Walter, there was no *way* I could jump far enough to reach the drainpipe, much less cling to the side of it.

I was a pretty unathletic guy.

Well, no, that was putting it too mildly. Imagine a bowl of pudding. Now imagine a boy who is as athletic as that bowl of pudding. That was me. Which meant I had to be creative sometimes.

"Kennedy, is there anything in that Dumpster?" I asked, motioning behind her. Kennedy frowned, then hurried to the Dumpster. She lugged out a few garbage bags, crinkling her nose at them.

"Do I want to know what's in those?" I asked, looking at the fat black bags through the chain-link fence.

Kennedy untied the top of one and made a face. "Probably not."

"Great. Put them in a pile for me?" I heaved myself onto the hood of the delivery truck.

"You're going to jump over the fence and straight into those bags?" Walter asked as I rolled up onto the roof like a loose potato. I found my footing and stood.

"Nope. I can't jump that far."

"You're going to hot-wire the truck and move it closer?" Walter asked, sounding excited.

"No— Well, I guess I could, but with the angles of the alley, I don't know if I can maneuver the truck closer, anyhow."

"You're going to—"

"You're going to throw me," I interrupted.

Walter's eyes went wide. He looked at the pile of trash bags, then back at me, then at the trash bags again. "What if I miss?" he asked hesitantly.

"Don't," I said. "And we're already at six minutes, so we need to move. Come on—I'll run and jump. I just need you to throw me to make up the difference, is all."

This was a sentence I'd never really imagined myself saying.

Kennedy shoved a bunch of the trash bags close together. Walter stood just beside me and gripped my arms. (Did his *fingers* lift weights? Because no one should have muscular *fingers*, but Walter Quaddlebaum did.) I took a deep breath and counted to three, and we charged forward across the top of the delivery truck. My foot hit the edge, I pushed off, and Walter shoved me upward and farther into the air. The barbed wire fence passed beneath me, and I had just enough time to see Kennedy's fearful expression as I came down. I smashed into the garbage bags. One broke, and something leaked out of it onto my feet. I wanted to get up, since that was pretty disgusting, but my body seemed to feel that if I was going to allow myself to be thrown over a fence, I deserved to be frozen for a few moments.

"Hale!" Kennedy squealed, shaking my shoulders frantically. I blinked at the clouds above me and finally sat up, coughing. I was going to have a bruise on my . . . well. On my everywhere, probably.

"You okay?" Walter called out just before he jumped from the truck to the drainpipe to the ground, finishing it all up with a slick forward roll into standing.

"I'm fine," I said, wincing as I stood and dusted myself off (bad idea—now there was garbage juice on my hands). Walter lifted part of a banana peel off my shoulder and tossed it away. "Let's move," I said and limped toward the door by the Dumpsters.

Step 2: Go through a locked door

Kennedy and Walter looked on while I grabbed what appeared to be one of those bingo-stampers from my belt. I stamped a large circle of red dots on the door with it. Nothing happened for a few beats, but then with a bright hiss, the dots caught fire and ate at the metal. We had to step back to avoid the flames, but when they finally died down, I nodded to Walter, who gave the circle a solid kick right in the center. The metal broke away and clattered to the ground.

"Door one—seven minutes, forty-three seconds—and remind me to talk to Ben about the amount of fire that thing puts out," I said, checking my watch. I led the way through the door and into the building. Kennedy and Walter immediately turned and walked sideways, so we had eyes in all directions. Outside, we were pretty safe—even if we didn't make it into the building, we weren't in any serious trouble. But inside? Guards, alarms, trip wires, cameras . . . It was dangerous in here.

Step 3: Navigate to the central computer

The hallway was lit by a handful of flickering, bug-filled fluorescent lights. There were dozens of doors—all locked—on either side, but I knew where we were headed; I'd been up since before dawn going over the building's blueprints. Walter and Kennedy, much to their dismay, had been woken up *at* dawn to go on the mission with me. But hey, everyone's always breaking into places under the cover of darkness. I'd figured morning light meant we had the element of surprise, *and* that only a handful of the building's occupants would be awake.

We made our way down the hall, right turn, left turn, third right, and eventually found ourselves peering through the windows of double doors leading into a space that looked like it may have been a conference hall at one point. On the opposite end of the room was a tower of beeping, flashing, outdated technology. The central computer—the thing we'd come for. I scanned the ceiling. Four cameras, all swiveling around seemingly at random. I knew the patterns, though—I'd taken an identical model apart ages ago, and the camera movements weren't random, exactly. Each was just following one of four complex patterns. It wasn't the most sophisticated system, but they got the job done.

"Door three," I said under my breath. "Eleven minutes, fifty-one seconds. Ready?"

Kennedy sprang up onto Walter's shoulders and stood tall and perfectly balanced—he was her reluctant cheerleading partner, so this was a well-practiced move for them. Walter held my sister's left ankle with one hand and then put his other on my shoulder to stay close. The cameras had very, very few blind spots, and the ones they did have were only a few feet wide. To stay hidden, we had to take up as little horizontal space as possible, which meant Kennedy on Walter's shoulders and Walter right behind me. I pushed the doors open, and we crept in.

I jumped across the floor, Walter immediately—and I mean *immediately*—behind me. Hopped to this tile, then

6

across, then *one, two, three*, then back, and *duck*. Our legs lifted and we pushed off the floor in perfect time—it was like a dance. A really, really weird dance. Kennedy was using one arm to hug her hair to her neck so stray pieces wouldn't be seen when camera three's view swept just over her head. I held my breath, worried about the alarm—if Kennedy had grown even a half inch in the last few weeks, the camera would see her . . .

Nope. The camera cleared us; I nodded, and off we went again, *one, two—big jump—three*, pause for a count of four—*move*.

Finally we slid behind the central computer, which was bulky enough to hide us from the cameras. Kennedy flipped off Walter's back and spun to the side to keep a lookout.

Step 4: Get the hard drives

"Time?" I asked as I grabbed a screwdriver off my belt. Walter took it from my hand and immediately began unscrewing the computer chassis.

"Thirteen minutes," Kennedy answered after checking her neon pink watch. The second hand was shaped like a unicorn and was circling a garden of rainbow-colored flowers. Walter finished up with the chassis cover and heaved it to the side. The two of us coughed in unison as a thick layer of dust rolled out at us.

"I can't believe they're still using this piece of junk," Walter said, hacking.

"It still works, though," I said and reached in. I grabbed a handful of wires and unplugged them. The first hard drive slid out easily, but the second jammed. I frowned, tugged harder—was it glued in? I fought with it for a moment, then yanked *hard*.

The room fell dark.

It was quick. One loud click and everything shut off, even the central computer. Walter pressed close; I heard Kennedy crack her knuckles, bracing for whatever was coming next. I took a deep breath.

A net dropped down from the darkness, startling all three of us. It pinned us to the ground; we smashed around one another, looking for the edges, but mostly there was just a bunch of kicks to the stomach and elbows to the chin. I winced as Walter—who was panicking a bit—thrashed around and walloped my nose.

The lights came back on.

They did so one at a time, hissing and popping as the power returned to the room. I looked around, assessing the situation—Kennedy was a mass of red hair. Walter was curled into a ball. High-stress situations didn't bring out the best in him.

The double doors swung open hard enough that they bounced off the back walls.

A man walked through. He was short and balding and looked kind of murderous. This was impressive because he was wearing pajamas, which don't really lend themselves to looking murderous, but Agent Otter could probably make an Easter Bunny costume look scary. He crossed his arms and glowered at the three of us.

"Nice try," he growled. "You made it farther than you did last time."

Two more figures appeared behind him—a boy and a girl, about my age. Ben's hair was sticking up in the back, and Beatrix, his twin, had pillow lines on her face.

"What was the time, Kennedy?" Beatrix asked.

"Sixteen minutes flat!" Kennedy answered triumphantly. Ben hurried over to the net we were trapped under and pressed his palm into the flat disks that were holding it to the floor.

"Cool, huh?" Ben said, his voice groggy with sleep. "They're magnetized! And the magnets reverse when I press them a certain way—" The magnet suddenly gave in, just as the boy had promised. The net went slack, and with a little fumbling, Kennedy, Walter, and I climbed out.

"What did we trip?" I asked the three newcomers, pausing to adjust the rear of my bodysuit. That's right. Bodysuit. I was wearing black spandex by choice these days, because it *was* a pretty effective outfit for spy work, no matter how ridiculous it made me look.

"Beatrix and I installed a fake hard drive last week. Drive two, I think?" Ben said, thumbing toward his sister and grinning. "When you grabbed it, it tripped the power grid and rang an alarm in the dorms. A really, really loud alarm—we weren't going to sleep through it like last time."

"You wired something to trip the *entire* League power grid without telling me?" the bald man interrupted. He was growling again, but I'd known Agent Otter long enough to know that was just his voice.

"Sorry," Ben said a little meekly.

I shook my head. "Don't be sorry. That was genius, Ben. The fewer people who know about the traps we set, the fewer chances for a security leak. The BENgo worked great, by the way," I finished, motioning to the bingo-stamper device we'd used on the exterior door. Ben wrote his name into *all* his inventions' titles, so no one else could claim to have made them.

"So we did it, then?" Walter asked. He still looked a little shaken from that business with the net and the darkness.

Everyone's eyes turned to me. They were all watching, waiting for an answer. It was hard to think back to a few months ago, when most people were looking at me for a quick laugh at the fat kid's expense. Now they were all waiting for me to nod. To say yes. To say that we'd finally finished after months of trying to turn an office full of outdated equipment into an elite security system that even SRS-trained agents couldn't break through.

I took a deep breath.

Step 5: Prove The League's security system
is SRS-agent-proof

I grinned. "Mission accomplished, everyone."

CHAPTER TWO

Here's a secret: life was easier at SRS.

I mean, it was and it wasn't. See, at SRS, I never questioned who I was. I was Hale Jordan, resident fat kid and wannabe field agent. My parents were SRS's top two agents. They were the good guys. The only thing between a world of innocent, unknowing citizens and The League, the world's most dangerous spy organization. I'd spent my entire life training, practicing, and studying, so one day I could be an agent—one of the good guys—just like my parents.

Of course, at SRS I was also known as Fail Hale, which wasn't easy, not by a long shot. And I was kind of a loser. And I was probably *never* going to get to be a field agent, since I couldn't pass the stupid physical exam.

But still—I knew who I was.

Then everything got turned upside down. I discovered that SRS were secretly the bad guys. The League were secretly the good guys. And my parents were stuck in the middle—on the run to keep from getting offed by SRS while also working to take them down completely, just like The League and I were.

But what did that all make me, exactly? I was a League agent now, sort of. I was in charge of my sister now, sort of. I was a spy now, sort of. And that last one was what I had always wanted, right? So it was wrong and terrible of me to feel, well . . .

Confused, I guess. Because as much as I hated SRS for everything they'd done—the lies, the crimes, putting a hit out on my parents—I still *missed* SRS. I missed my old life.

I missed my parents.

But, I reminded myself whenever I missed them too much, *they're heroes—they walked away from SRS, from everything they've ever known, from their family, because it was the right thing to do. Nothing's ever easy for heroes. That's why there are so few heroes—and why it's so great that your parents are two of them. That's why you need to work harder to be one too, instead of wallowing around missing SRS like some sort of . . . wallower. Stop whining, you wallower. Stop it!*

"Are you ready?" someone asked from my door—Walter. I sat up in bed to see him looking my room over, frowning. "Seriously, man. You've got to put up some posters or some . . . something."

"What would I put up posters of?" I asked.

"I don't know. Cars. Sports teams. Bikini girls."

I lifted my eyebrows.

"Okay, then, wiring schematics for SRS-localized missile-launch controllers. Just *something*. Your room is depressing," Walter said, rolling his eyes at me. I ignored him, ducking to grab my shoes from under my bed. The truth was, Walter was right. We were all living at League headquarters now, and everyone else's rooms were decorated. Kennedy's was covered in neon cartoon animals and nine billion shades of pink. Walter's was covered in posters of the stuff he'd mentioned earlier—cars, sports teams, and bikini girls—even though I knew he had a stuffed frog hidden under his blankets. Ben's was full of wires and pictures of Nikola Tesla. Beatrix's was full of spare computer parts. Even Otter's room was probably decorated, though who knows what with—I didn't want to think too hard about what Otter looked at as he fell asleep at night.

And mine was white. White walls, white bedspread, white floor.

When we left SRS for good last year, I hadn't thought to take anything with me. In my head there wasn't *time*. I'd been so caught up in getting myself, Walter, and Kennedy out that I hadn't thought about taking *things*. Walter, however, had remembered to pack his stuffed frog, some T-shirts, and a telescope his parents gave him. Kennedy had grabbed her favorite set of pom-poms, a few photos of Mom and Dad, and Mom's wedding ring.

I didn't have anything. I mean, I had *them*, and I knew that should have been enough, but still. I wish I'd grabbed something. Like one of Dad's ties, or maybe his grappling hook set . . .

See? Wallowing again.

"You're going to be late," Walter said, nodding at my alarm clock.

"That's four minutes fast," I said. "And besides, what's Otter going to do—give me pushups?"

Walter grinned as I finished tying my shoes. I joined him at the door, and together we walked down the hall and upstairs to The League's mission control room.

Mission control was looking good these days. Or better, anyhow. We'd spent ages sourcing old television sets and video equipment, Frankenstein-ing computers together under Beatrix's careful eye, and now we had a pretty decent control center. It still smelled a little like corn chips, but to be fair, most of the building did. Otter was sitting at a giant metal desk in the back of the room, poring over papers and maps and folders, while my sister and Clatterbuck—Stan Clatterbuck, to be specific, who was Beatrix and Ben's uncle—raced around in rolling chairs. Beatrix was at the command desk, typing hurriedly on her Right Hand, her name for a device that looked like three cell phones welded together but had more computing power than anything else in the building. Ben, meanwhile, was sketching something on a legal pad, face mashed into hard, thoughtful lines.

"What's that?" I asked as we walked up.

"The BENdy Straw," Ben said triumphantly, showing me the drawing. It looked like some sort of camera device on a wire, but you never could tell with his inventions. Sometimes stuff that looked like, say, a plastic boat, wound up being a miniature flamethrower. Walter learned that the hard way, when he went to play with the aforementioned plastic boat and lost three-fourths of his eyebrows.

"You're going to run out of words that have 'Ben' in them, eventually. You know that, right?" Kennedy said, rising from her rolling chair after thoroughly trouncing Clatterbuck. She'd traded her black spy suit for a fluffy pink skirt and a shirt with a cartoon dog wearing sunglasses. Ben either ignored or didn't hear her because he was busy writing "The BENdy Straw" across the top of the paper.

"All right, all right—we're all here?" Otter grumbled, like he wanted to get this meeting over with as soon as possible. Everyone gathered around the desk.

"All right, boss man," Clatterbuck said warmly. "What's our next move?"

Our. That was the thing that made life here at The League worth it, even if it wasn't *easier.* SRS might have been a team, sure, but here? We were an "us."

Otter cleared his throat, like Clatterbuck's enthusiasm grossed him out. "Well. I've gone over all the information we've collected. And now that we have our own security sorted out, I think it's time we strike SRS. See if we can knock them down a little further." He waved to some papers on the desk, like we were supposed to make sense of them. "Now, we can't best them with manpower or artillery or influence. But what we *can* do is make sure they don't get any more of these things. Which is why we're going to hit them where it hurts. We're taking their money."

We collectively blinked at Otter. Finally Beatrix said, "We're going to rob them?"

"We're going to rob their bank account," Otter corrected. He pointed to a sheet of paper—it was a printout of some fancy-looking building. "This is the Central Bank of Switzerland. It's where SRS stores their wealth—some in cash, some in digital accounts, and some in gold bars."

"How much money are we talking about?" I asked curiously.

Otter shrugged. "Between all three? Around ninety million. They have smaller accounts in Russia and Thailand, but this is their heart, money-wise. If we try anything else—stopping a mission, say, or interrupting their operations, they'll just be able to spring right back up so long as this account exists. We'll be playing spy Whac-A-Mole for the rest of our lives. But I happen to know the fake name they use for their bank accounts: Antonio Halfred."

"How do you know that?" Walter asked. "You weren't in accounting."

Otter looked indignant. "I dated an agent in accounting—"

"You dated Agent Bullwhipple?" Kennedy squealed, though I couldn't tell if it was in horror or delight. Having once accidentally caught Agent Bullwhipple tweezing her mustache at her desk, *I* was particularly horrified.

Otter slapped his notebook to calm the chatter that had erupted over the room. "My private dating life is irrelevant! My point is, we know the name. Once we're in Switzerland, we'll sort out how to pose as Antonio Halfred and—"

"We're going to Switzerland?" Beatrix shouted, and she and Kennedy jumped around in a circle together. Ben and Walter high-fived—

"Not for vacation! We're going for work!" Otter roared, looking like he wished he'd stayed in bed today.

"How are we even going to get ninety million dollars back into the country?" I asked. Even though we were a government agency, we operated more or less on our own—the government, after all, didn't want to admit to 1) having a secret spy agency or 2) the fact that there was a *second* secret spy agency, a bad one, that they couldn't stop.

Otter said, "I'm thinking that rather than sneak it back in, we just open our own Swiss bank account. Transfer the money from their account to ours."

"We could afford new computers!" I said, getting excited. "And to run the air-conditioning all summer without dimming the lights! We'll be a real spy agency again!"

"Hey!" Clatterbuck said.

"It'll be enough that we can bring in some real agents too," Otter said.

"Hey!" Walter said.

"Come on, Walter," I said. "Let's be real—it'd be nice to have some actual funding here. Think about how long it took us to set up a decent security system, what with the ancient cameras and all."

"I was thinking about how we *did* set up a great security system *despite* the ancient cameras," Walter said darkly, and to my surprise, Kennedy, Beatrix, and Ben all nodded in agreement. Clatterbuck was staring at the ground, since he was a little wary of confrontation, but I could tell he agreed too.

"Seriously? Guys, we can do a lot more good if we're not worrying about keeping the lights on," I said.

Kennedy spoke up. "But . . . Hale. All that money belongs to SRS."

"Yes. That's why we should take it," I said impatiently.

"No, you don't get it—it belongs to SRS. Which means they probably got it by doing something terrible. That money is . . . Well. It's . . . *bad*," Kennedy said. And she was right, of course—SRS made their money in some pretty terrible ways. Black market deals. Robberies. Heists. Ransom payments.

Still, I shook my head. "Money is money. Whatever SRS did to earn it, it's done. Besides, isn't it better that we do something *good* with that money, to undo the bad?"

"Yes. I think we should give it away. To charity," Walter said, his voice a little uncertain.

"Oh, good idea," Ben said. "There's this space camp that would be really grateful—"

"We're not *giving away* millions of dollars while we're eating five-dollar pizzas every night," Otter scoffed. "We're spies, not Robin Hood and his army."

"Robin Hood had a gang of thieves, not an army," Beatrix said. Otter glared, and Beatrix shrank down. The room fell into stony, uneasy silence, save the dusty whir of old computer fans. I looked at Kennedy; she was studying the owl stickers on her boots intently, which was something she did when she didn't agree with me.

I exhaled. Maybe they had a point, and that money was dirty—money earned stealing and hurting and destroying and conning. That didn't make much sense to me, to be honest, but . . . well. Maybe I was thinking too much like an SRS agent. Maybe if I were a better League agent, I would agree with them more, right?

You want to be a hero, don't you, Hale? Like your parents? I said to myself. I closed my eyes and tried not to daydream too hard about the air-conditioning working all summer.

"All right," I said, exhaling. "All right—how about we get the money. We see how much it is. And then we take what we *have* to have to cover the basics, and everything else, we give away to that space camp."

"We are *not giving money to a space camp!*" Otter roared. His head was flushed red and purple, like a giant grape.

"We'll decide once we have it!" I said firmly.

Otter stared at me, then at the others, then back at me.

"I like Hale's idea," Kennedy said.

"Me too," Ben answered. The others chimed in one at a time, except Clatterbuck, who seemed torn between the promise of new computers and space camp. Finally he shrugged at Otter.

"No harm in waiting to make a choice," he said. Clatterbuck wasn't much of a spy, but as the only other adult in the room, his words shut down Otter's argument in a way the rest of ours couldn't.

"Fine," Otter snipped. "Fine, fine, fine. We'll decide once we've got the money. Which means we have to get the money. Nine hundred hours tomorrow, everyone. We've got to figure out how to get to Switzerland."

Otter spun around and stomped out of the room, talking about "superior officers" and "subordination" and a few other *s* words I didn't understand but that definitely weren't pleasant. Kennedy and Beatrix bounded away together, and soon Ben and Clatterbuck were off to begin salvaging parts of the BENdy Straw ("Do you think it'll be bad if we take the hoses from the sinks on the fourth floor?"), leaving me and Walter alone on the command deck.

"Switzerland," Walter said. "Our first foreign assignment as real agents! Are you nervous?"

"No. You?"

"Well, it does . . . Well. It does sort of feel like I'm stealing from my mom," Walter said, toeing at the ground.

"Yeah."

That was a pretty dumb thing to say—"Yeah"—but I didn't know what else *to* say. Walter and I never talked about his mom these days. We never talked about how she was still at SRS. We never wondered if she still believed SRS were the good guys, or if she was siding with them despite knowing they were the bad guys. We never wondered if she missed Walter, and I never asked if he missed her. I never asked if he forgave her for staying at SRS. It wasn't that I wasn't curious about all that—I *was*—it was just . . . Well. I didn't know how to start the conversation, I guess.

So we just didn't talk about it.

CHAPTER THREE

Switzerland wasn't as cold as I expected.

I mean, you think Switzerland, you think snow, right? And there was snow—on the mountains—but Geneva itself was pretty mild, like Castlebury in early fall. It was Kennedy's, Beatrix's, and Ben's first time out of the country; Walter and I had been to London with our parents when we were seven or so while they were doing some undercover work (they never told me the specifics, but I remember Mom spent a lot of time in a palace guard costume). I wouldn't have admitted it out loud, but I was trying to play it casual, like I was unfazed by world travel, because I didn't want to 1) draw attention to myself, 2) remind Otter how inexperienced I was, or 3) look like Clatterbuck, who was wearing a big, floppy hat and taking photos of everything from the sidewalks to the street signs.

But despite my best attempts, I *was* thrown by how amazingly pretty Geneva was. Like, calendar-photo beautiful. Desktop-of-your-computer beautiful. How the Swiss didn't just walk around, mouths hanging open, I couldn't understand. When no one else was looking, I urged Clatterbuck to take a few photos of the place where the sky met the lake—it looked like the entire world was the same shade of bright, cartoony blue. He obliged, but then got too close and fell *in* the lake. The Swiss guys who fished him out said it happened all the time, but I'm pretty sure they were just being nice.

We set about learning everything we could about the Central Bank of Switzerland. Some of the information we needed was easy enough—the guard rotations, for example, which we got by hanging around the bank building like confused tourists and cataloging each moment a guard left his shift. The floor plans were easy to get too—they were on file with the local building commissioner, and with a little hacking on Beatrix's part, we were able to get access without arousing any suspicion.

But the tricky part—well, the *nearly* impossible part—was getting SRS's actual account number. Without the account number, we couldn't find their vault. Breaking in and robbing the bank was impossible if we didn't even know where in the building we were looking.

Mission: Get SRS's account number
Step 1: Play dress-up

We didn't exactly have the money to buy designer cloth-ing for our cover story, but luckily, The League had some fancy clothes from the 1970s in storage. They looked . . . well. I wouldn't say they looked *good*, but they were expen-sive when they were bought and had been around long enough that the styles were vintage cool rather than out-dated gross. Otter was wearing sunglasses and a suit with stripes and had slicked his hair back in a way that accen-tuated the bald spot on the crown of his head. Kennedy looked pretty acceptable in this weird red dress with swoopy sleeves and cheetahs running around the hem—I think it was supposed to be a short dress on an adult, but on her, it passed for a drapey long one. And me?

The League never had kid agents like SRS did, which meant none of the clothing fit me. Ben actually knew how to work a sewing machine, given the number of fabric-related inventions he'd made, so he tried to cut down a suit for me to wear. Except the jacket turned out all wrong, which meant I was currently wearing pale green suit pants with a sort of punk T-shirt we'd found in the storage box. Beatrix called it rocker chic. I called it legs-eaten-by-a-frog chic.

But hey, rich people always dress weird, right? And that was our cover—a rich man and his two kids. More specifi-cally, Antonio Halfred and his two kids.

The bank was a giant old building, the sort that had placards everywhere talking about how this wall or that painting or that ceiling was built a billion years ago. The exterior was magnificent—all bright-white marble and columns so fat that four or five people could easily hide behind one. The doors were strange and modern by comparison—automatic revolving doors that I managed to get stuck in, because of course I did.

Inside, the ceiling stretched high above us, arching at the top, where a chandelier hung amid elaborate gold ceiling panels. There were windows created in the swoops and curves where the ceiling met the walls, which let in light that bounced happily off sleekly polished wooden floors. Straight ahead was a long row of bankers at wooden desks set behind glass, and on either end was a smattering of offices with open doors and big windows, where people typed furiously at their computers. Otter held his head high and clacked his dress shoes across the marble floor to the nearest banker. He flipped his chrome-shiny sunglasses up on top of his gel-shiny hair. The banker—a pretty girl with ultrablond hair—looked up at him and smiled.

"Hey there," he said in a flirty voice, and winked at the banker. I wondered if it would be impolite to throw up in the bank?

"Hello, sir. How can I help you?" she said with a smidge of a Swiss accent and eyes that said, *Nice try, man, but no.*

Otter looked a bit crestfallen for a moment, but he bounced back. "I'd like to make a deposit into my account."

"Of course. We'll need your identification and account number," said the banker—LEONIE, according to her name tag.

Step 2: Get behind the desk

This was my and Kennedy's cue—to start getting bored. I exhaled, like this entire trip was just *too much*, and began to kick my shoes at the ground. Leonie glanced at me, but Otter had her attention again within the second.

"Here's my ID, but I'm afraid I've forgotten the account number and lost my deposit slips. So many banks and countries to keep track of . . ." Otter said, and fished a fake Antonio Halfred passport from his pocket. As Otter removed the passport, he let a few stubs from a nearby horse race spill across the counter—pocket litter we'd planted to subtly seal the "rich guy" cover. Leonie noticed them as she took the passport and then typed a few things into the computer. Meanwhile, Kennedy and I continued being bored, until finally I pulled out a phone and began playing a game. Kennedy, who didn't have a phone, wandered forward, pretending to play hopscotch along the floor tiles. Leonie glanced over at her.

"I'm in a bit of a rush," Otter said politely. Kennedy continued to hopscotch.

Leonie looked back to Otter. "All right, Monsieur—er, Mister—Halfred . . . Let's see . . . Yes, here we are. You wanted to make a deposit?"

"Indeed, just a bit from my winnings. I won't be able to take this back to the US without having to declare the money at customs. More trouble than it's worth!" Otter said. Then to me, "Georgie—son, fetch your sister!"

I groaned dramatically. And while Otter held most of Leonie's attention, I stomped over to grab ahold of Kennedy's arm.

Step 3: Get a picture of the computer screen with the account number

All I needed was a decent image of the monitor. Beatrix could blow it up later so we could read the account number. While I bickered with Kennedy quietly, I casually tilted the phone, positioning my fingers to snap the photo.

Leonie was in the way.

She was sitting slightly off to one side, and her shoulder was blocking the screen. I tried again, but no luck—then she glanced back at me, so I had no choice but to grab Kennedy's arm.

"Hey!" Kennedy whined, and we began to retreat to Otter. I made eye contact with him and shook my head quickly, letting him know we needed more time.

"The deposit, mademoiselle?" Otter said slickly, drawing Leonie's attention back to him.

"Yes, Mr. Halfred—it looks like this account is flagged. Only one of my coworkers, Markus Hastings, can deal with the account." She said Markus Hastings's name like he was a slug or centipede or something else people pretty much universally wanted to squish.

"You mean, *you* can't help me?" Otter said, turning up the charm again. I added him to the list of things people wanted to squish.

"No," Leonie said politely. "Just let me give Markus a call, though. He'll be right down."

Leonie picked up the phone at her desk and then ran her finger along an employee directory taped to the wood below it. She stopped her finger and then dialed. Kennedy and I were passing the desk now. I still didn't have a clear shot of the number.

I hooked my foot into the corner of the desk and tripped forward. I released Kennedy's arm and, on the way down, grabbed the desk for support. I missed, though, and wound up grabbing the phone. Me, the phone, some paperwork, and three pencils careened into the floor. Leonie gasped, and a few people nearby spun around to see what the commotion was about. I could feel my knee swelling and rug burn spreading down my shins. I groaned and sat up—

"Are you all right?" Leonie asked in French, so stunned that she had forgotten to speak in English. I looked at her blankly, even though I understood, until she repeated the question in English.

"I'm fine," I said as Otter fussed over me and then hauled me to my feet. Everyone—even a non-spy—can spot a fake trip a mile away, so I'd had to really go for it. I groaned and rubbed the spot on my head that had crashed into the side of the desk, while Kennedy pranced around me, snickering.

"You should have seen your face, Georgie!" she hooted. Leonie gave Kennedy a stern look, and Otter grabbed for her but she dodged away. Leonie was trying to look after me, silently scold Kennedy, and gather her things all at once. I reached over and quickly, easily, yanked at the plug connecting her phone to the ground socket. It popped out neatly.

"Well—let's see. Er, Markus. Right," Leonie said, shaking her head as she put her pencils back in her desk. She lifted the phone again and then frowned. "It's not working," she said, hanging it up and trying again.

"Did he break it?" Otter said, sounding disgruntled. "You must be more careful, son."

"I didn't mean to fall on my face!" I said, flushing.

"You'll have to pay for it," Otter said, shaking his head.

"But it was an accident!" I wailed. "It wouldn't have even happened if stupid Violetta hadn't gone over there and you didn't make me go get her—"

"It's no trouble," Leonie interrupted. She smiled at me sympathetically. "These things happen. You won't need to pay for the phone. But you'll have to excuse me, since I'll need to dash upstairs to get Markus for you."

"Fine," Otter said. "But hurry please. Like I said, we're in a rush. I need to get this deposited before my son breaks anything else." He waved an envelope—which we'd stuffed with clipped coupons, since we didn't have hundreds of dollars—in the air. Leonie looked hurt on my behalf and then scurried away.

"I can't believe you broke her phone," Otter said. "Really, Georgie. See if you can fix it." No one could hear this, but it would be a decent show for the security officers if they were watching us. I rolled my eyes and fidgeted with the phone for a minute, then pulled on the cord. I lifted it to show Otter—and the security cameras—it was unplugged, and then circled Leonie's desk. I jammed the phone cord back into its socket and, as I rose, snapped a picture of the computer screen. We didn't have time to check it—there was no telling how close or far Markus Hastings's desk was from Leonie's. I made eye contact with Otter. *I've got the photo.*

Otter shoved his hands in his pockets, looking bored. We couldn't just bolt for the door; it would attract attention. He waited another beat and then lifted his cell phone—which didn't even work—to answer an imaginary call.

"What? No! Tell the pilot we'll be there momentarily. My god, I pay his salary—he'll wait there all day if I want him to!" Otter grunted into the phone. He rolled his eyes, looked at the envelope of "money" in his hands, then at Leonie's empty desk. "Fine, we're on our way. Let's move, kids," he said to us as he stormed off. We followed behind, Kennedy still hopscotching. A few other bankers looked up as we stomped through the doors, but their faces said, *What a rich jerk!* rather than *Oh no, spies!* so I didn't panic. I turned back to look just as Otter and Kennedy breezed through the door.

There was Leonie, at the top of the staircase, with a man who I assumed was Markus Hastings. I couldn't tell you a thing about his height or weight or even his hair, because in the split second our eyes met, all I really noticed was this: Markus Hastings looked terrified.

And terrified people? They're the most dangerous.

CHAPTER FOUR

The place where we were staying in Geneva was really nice. This was pretty surprising, since we couldn't exactly *pay* for a fancy hotel or anything. But apparently, Clatterbuck's old spy days meant he and The League still *did* have contacts around the world. His contacts, however, were a little different than what I expected. When the SRS says it has contacts, they mean oil barons and CEOs and mob bosses. Clatterbuck's contact? A farmer.

Well, technically a horse breeder. Small horses. Or rather, (in French), *poneys.*

The miniature-horse breeder—a very old man and his wife—had a house on their property they rented out to travelers, and Clatterbuck secured it for us for three weeks. ("If all this SRS business takes longer than that, maybe we can offer to feed the horses to stay?") Unfortunately, the old couple spoke only Romansh, which was the only language in Switzerland I *didn't* know. Neither did Clatterbuck, so we made do with lots of smiling and thumbs-ups to convey our gratitude.

"And how do you know them, again?" Otter asked. He was so amazed, I think he forgot to look irritated.

"I had to go in disguise as a circus animal trainer once. They lent me the ponies," Clatterbuck said. "I guess you could say we hit it off."

"But . . . you don't even speak the same language," Beatrix said, shaking her head.

"No, but I brought them chocolate and made the bed when I left. It went a long way," Clatterbuck said happily, like this explained everything. He turned and went into the house, leaving the rest of us outside, staring at the darkened forms of a tiny pony herd nosing its way up to the barn for dinner.

Inside was sparse but pretty—lots of white tile on the floors and the walls. Beds with perfectly square foam pillows and neatly tucked-in blankets. Bathrooms with windows that overlooked the aforementioned ponies—I guess so you could pee and observe nature all at once. The art on the wall was weird, but not too terrible, even though Kennedy did take down the creepy painting of an old lady that was in the bedroom she and Beatrix were sharing. ("It *stares* at us, Hale. Can paintings be haunted?") Walter, Ben, and I were in another room that had four bunk beds—just enough room for three boys and all of Ben's inventing equipment.

We convened at the kitchen table, pulling up an extra recliner and barstool so there was enough room for the seven of us. Beatrix had her Right Hand out and plugged into two different computers. We watched as she pulled up my photo of the bank code and stabilized it, snatching the number off the screen. She then went through a series of screens that contained about a billion numbers and letters, typing frantically. Finally she looked up at us.

She was frowning.

"What's wrong?" I asked.

Beatrix kept frowning. "There's about three dollars and four cents in the account. Adjusting for the currency exchange rate, of course."

We blinked.

"Maybe this doesn't account for the hard cash and the gold in the vaults, is all," Otter said swiftly.

"No—this is *including* what's in the vaults rather than in the digital account. Three dollars and four cents."

"That's impossible," I said, shaking my head. "We hurt SRS when we broke out of the Castlebury location, but we didn't ruin their finances. Besides, SRS would never allow the money to get so low. They must have moved it."

"Well, wait—no . . . Hang on, it's weird," Beatrix said, typing frantically again. "All right—so, yes, money was moved out of this account. It was moved to another account that has . . . a hundred thousand in it. And then last week, money was moved from that account to two different accounts. And those were moved to . . . three others. Hang on, I'm getting confused by the trail."

"That doesn't make any sense," Otter said. "Antonio Halfred, that's the name—did you type it in right?"

"I did," Beatrix answered testily. "I'm telling you, if this is SRS's account, they've moved the money recently. They're moving it a *lot*."

"Well, sure, moving it makes sense—it'd keep people like us from being able to find it. But that couldn't have been *all* of SRS's money. Even if that account had a hundred thousand dollars in it at one point, SRS has *millions*. Where is *that* money?" Walter asked.

We went quiet again.

And then I realized. I exhaled. "It's . . . everywhere."

"What do you mean?" Kennedy asked.

"Beatrix—can you see how many accounts SRS's money has been in? Or how many are connected in some way to this Antonio Halfred?" I asked.

"Uh, well, I can try? But I won't be able to see them all. There are hundreds. Maybe more," Beatrix said.

"Probably thousands," I said. I leaned back in my chair, nearly tilting over when the legs slid on the tile. "SRS spreads their resources out. There are dozens of facilities. Even more sleeper agents throughout the world. They have their hands in organized crime and medicines and real estate. Of course they'd spread out their money too."

"They have their money in thousands of accounts," Otter said, nodding in realization. "And they move it around so no one catches it."

"Are these accounts all in Antonio Halfred's name?" Walter asked.

"No," Beatrix said. "They're in a bunch of other people's. And they seem to be real people too. This account I'm looking at now belongs to a butcher. This other one belongs to a lady who owns a shoe store."

"Genius," I said. "Hide some money in real people's accounts for a week or two. If they notice, they won't say anything—who complains about an extra thousand or so in their bank account? And it means there's no way to steal *just* the SRS money—the accounts are always changing. The amounts are always changing. I bet even the vaults are always changing. No wonder the account is tied to that Hastings guy—he must handle all this for them."

"He's their inside man. We have to get past SRS *and* the bank's security *and* someone at the bank who actually knows what's going on with those accounts," I said, slumping down in my chair. I stared at the smooth wood tabletop. No one moved. Everyone waited for someone else in the room to have the great idea.

But no one did.

"So we're done? We can't do it?" Kennedy asked, frowning.

"Looks that way," Otter said. He stood up, his chair clattering behind him. He stomped off to his bedroom, which Clatterbuck had the misfortune of sharing with him, and slammed the door.

Ben snored.

Ben *really* snored. Like, the sort of snoring that sounds like a truck on the interstate. It was kind of incredible that such a spectacular sound could come from a guy so small. I tossed and turned on the lower bunk, trying to figure out if Walter, who was sleeping above me, was awake. Finally I just whispered up to him.

"Yeah, I'm awake," he grumbled. "I tried to smother myself with a pillow, but it didn't work. Maybe you could come knock me out?"

"You really want *me* punching you?" I answered, and Walter laughed under his breath. We went silent for a few more moments, which Ben graciously filled with a bunch of short snores all in a row.

"I'm sort of relieved about the bank. It's a big job," Walter finally said, his voice a little edgy, like he wasn't sure he was allowed to say this.

"You wouldn't have gone in alone or anything," I reassured him. Walter got jumpy on missions—he was the sort of guy who could rewire a light grid flawlessly in the practice room but would freeze up in the field.

"That wasn't really what I meant, actually," Walter said, his voice lower now. "I mean, it's a big job. SRS would be so angry. And they've still got my mom . . ."

I felt stupid for not realizing what he meant, so I scrambled. "Oh. Well. Your mom is tough as nails. They wouldn't be able to hurt her even if they wanted to. She'd go on the run."

"Like your parents?"

I was quiet for a long time, thinking, *No, not like my parents.* Because, see, my parents went on the run even though it meant *leaving* me and Kennedy, because getting out of SRS was the right thing to do—because they were heroes, and sometimes heroes had to do really hard things like that. Right? But Walter was already gone—his mom could just *leave.* She could walk out right now, and if anything, she'd be even closer to getting to be with Walter again—it'd practically be easy! Yet, she was staying with SRS. She was just choosing to stay with the bad guys.

I thought I could guess *why* she was staying. Because it was easier. She knew who she was at SRS—she knew the rules, the system, the goals. She didn't know who she'd be here on the outside. But if I could get out despite all that, then so could she, right?

Out loud, though, I finally said, "Yeah, I guess like my parents. They could join up, maybe. Help each other out.

And then when SRS is done for, we'll all go to some theme park together."

Walter laughed a little under his breath, sounding relieved that I'd finally said something. "You on a roller coaster. Sure, Hale. Sure."

"I let Ben strap inventions I don't understand to my belt every day. I promise you, I'm totally cool with a roller coaster," I answered, but I laughed too. Ben stopped snoring for a second, and I thought maybe we'd woken him up. We went still . . .

SNORE.

Walter and I laughed more, trying to keep quiet, but doing so only made my stomach muscles burn and twist, which made me laugh more. Finally we settled down, and Ben rolled over a little so he was snoring at the wall instead of right at us. I was sort of getting that black, dizzy feeling, about to fall asleep, when Walter spoke, his voice low again, like he hoped I was already out.

"I know you're mad that so many people stayed at SRS, Hale. But I think you—*we*—have to remember that SRS— *they're* the bad guys. They're the ones that used us, your parents, my mom, *everyone*—"

"Maybe Hastings," I said, frowning. "He looked really scared at the bank today—maybe he's not *helping* them so much as they're using him, just like they used us."

"Right, maybe. But what I'm saying is, I know you're

mad that so many people stayed, but sometimes, I think, it's just hard for people to do the right thing."

Hastings's face was still in my head, but I pushed it aside to answer Walter. "Of course it's hard. It was hard for my parents to leave me and Kennedy. But when you know it's the right thing, you have to do it."

"Right," Walter said quietly.

I looked at the bedsprings above me, thinking about Walter on the other side of them. Sometimes I think he wished I'd never told him the truth about SRS and The League.

Sometimes I wished I didn't know the truth either. But that's not the way the truth works—the truth doesn't care if you believe in it or know about it or like it. It doesn't care if sometimes you wish it would all go away, and that you could be back in apartment 300 with your mom and dad and sister like any normal superspy family.

Hard or scary or complicated, the truth is just the truth.

CHAPTER FIVE

"SRS used us. And I'm telling you, they're using Hastings too. He needs our help," I said firmly the next morning.

Otter looked at me like I was just as disappointing as the cup of instant coffee he was nursing. "First off, you don't *know* that, Jordan. You're just assuming because the guy looked nervous at the bank. Secondly, "used" doesn't mean the same thing as "threatened." Hastings probably knows exactly what he's doing for SRS—and is probably being paid very, very well for it."

"He didn't look *nervous*; he looked *scared*," I said. "Look, all I'm saying is, we go to his house. We see if he needs our help getting out of SRS. If not, we leave Geneva."

"After a helicopter tour?" Clatterbuck said wistfully from the kitchen.

"My hand to god, Clatterbuck, if you mention that helicopter tour *one more time* . . . ," Otter said through gritted teeth. He looked back to me. "And if he tells SRS about us coming to see him?"

"If he were going to tell SRS about us, he'd have done it yesterday," I pointed out.

"He's got a point," Walter said from across the table. Walter had his own instant coffee, but he wasn't drinking it. I think he just wanted to hold it and make himself look older.

Otter scowled. "All the more reason for us to leave *now*. We're not going to Hastings's house, and that's final."

We *were* going to Hastings's, though, because everyone else was on board with me, so Otter was outvoted. We used the Internet to find Hastings's home address. And then we went to his house. *All* of us, actually—Otter wanted to make it just himself, me, and Walter, but the others started complaining about being cooped up and wanting to *do* something and what did it matter if it wasn't really a *mission* so much as a visit to find out if Hastings was being used or paid? Otter relented, then went and lay down for a long time, because we "made him tired."

We all packed into a big orange-and-white public bus and rode it up to Hastings's neighborhood, just past the enormous lake on the northern edge of Geneva.

When we arrived at Hastings's address, I gave Otter a defeated look. It was the biggest house on the street, with a view of Lake Geneva and the Swiss Alps. It wasn't something a banker—even an upper-management sort of banker—could afford, which meant Otter was likely right—SRS *did* pay Hastings, and they paid him very, very well.

Walter reached the door first; he glanced back at us and then reached out and knocked hastily on it. It took a few moments, but then finally we heard shoes clapping on the floor. The door swung open.

"What do you want?" Hastings asked sharply in German.

"Er, ein . . . ein—no, wir—" Walter stumbled; languages had never been his forte. I stepped around Walter and squared my shoulders to Hastings.

"Wir möchten mit Ihnen reden," I said quickly. *We'd like to talk to you.*

Hastings gave me a confused look. His eyes danced over the seven of us, trying to sort out who we were. Then suddenly it clicked.

"You were at the bank!" he said in English, horrified. "You're from SRS—you used the code name, the Antonio Halfred name! What have I done? Did I do something wrong? Are you angry?"

Whoa—now I was convinced *I* was right after all, because Hastings looked like he might actually pass out from fear. I said, "No—that's the point. We're *not* with the Sub Rosa Society. We're with—"

Hastings's eyes widened, and his mouth dropped. He stepped back through his door and then tried to slam it, but I jammed my foot into the frame just before he could. I winced as the pressure of the door crushed my toes.

"We just want to talk!" I said. "We need to tell you—"

"You're going to ruin everything! Go away!" Hastings shouted.

Walter and Clatterbuck jumped forward and pressed on the door; when the two of them couldn't fling it open, Kennedy and Ben joined in. Otter stood in the back, looking somewhat more dignified than the rest of us.

Hastings's back was to the door, pressing it in on us. When Beatrix finally threw her slight weight against it, the door gave, and we all went crashing into Hastings's foyer, sliding across the marble floor in a heap. We tumbled into a fancy wooden table on the other side, breaking the wood and sending a bowl of fake lemons toppling to the ground. Hastings scrambled to his feet as the rest of us sorted out our limbs.

"You have to go!" Hastings said, turning to Otter—I supposed he seemed like the most reasonable one there.

"Believe me, I want to," Otter said drily. "But that one, there—the chubby one, yes—he insisted we talk to you. The faster the conversation, the faster we're gone."

I glowered at Otter's low shot but then turned to Hastings. Clatterbuck, Beatrix and Ben, and Walter walked over to stand behind me, while Kennedy walked up beside me and gave Hastings her friendliest smile. Hastings swallowed loudly. For the first time, I got a really solid look at him. He was short, and even though he was young and not exactly fat, he looked like he'd be about as useful in a relay race as I'd be. He'd brushed his hair messily to try to disguise the bald spot near the top of his head, and despite the fact that it was Saturday, was wearing a dress shirt—though he did have the sleeves rolled up.

Hastings smashed his lips together, and then said, "Fine. Fine. Come on. Let's get away from the windows, at least." He waved us all farther into the house, keeping his eyes especially firm on Clatterbuck and Otter, like he expected them to pull out weapons at any second. As we went along he jumped ahead, pulling drapes and closing shutters. The house was dim by the time we'd made it to a parlor in the back. On the walls there were fancy oil paintings of old ladies wearing furs and pearls, and all the sofas were the stiff, tufted kind. I sat down but then wished I hadn't— the cushions felt like embroidered rocks. There wasn't enough room, so Kennedy, Beatrix, and Ben all sat cross-legged on the floor.

"All right, Mr. Hastings, we'll be quick," I said. Hastings stood in the parlor door, fidgeting. Kennedy kept smiling at him, which clearly made him even more nervous.

"SRS—you're handling their money for them, right? Helping to keep it hidden?"

"Maybe," Hastings said, shrugging.

"Dude, come on. We obviously already know," Walter said, sighing.

I gave Walter a hard look. "Well, let's say *you are*," I continued, trying to be patient. "We just wanted to make sure you know exactly what SRS is. And if they're forcing you to help them, then we want to help *you* escape."

Hastings cracked his knuckles. "What are you, twelve? *Who* are you?"

"We're The League," Clatterbuck said, sounding proud—I could tell he'd been waiting a long time to say this again. Ben and Beatrix smiled at their uncle.

"The what?" Hastings asked, and Clatterbuck's face fell a little.

"We're an opposing spy organization from the States," Otter explained, his voice growly. "I'm the director. Ben and Beatrix are the tech team. Kennedy's the cat burglar. Walter's the right-hand man. Clatterbuck's the ways-and-means guy. Hale's the lead agent. We're the organization meant to stop SRS for good, and if you stop wasting our time, we can explain why you should help us instead of them."

"If you kill me, they'll know—"

"*Kill you?* Whoa, whoa, *whoa*," Beatrix said, waving her hands.

"We're not killing anyone. It's not really our thing," Ben said.

"We just wanted to make sure you're not in trouble, basically. That you don't need rescuing," Walter finished.

Markus let his eyes rest on each of us for a moment, and then he shook his head, wiped his face with his hand, and fidgeted some more. If it weren't his house, and if he were maybe a little more athletic, I was pretty certain he would've taken off running. I looked at everyone else. What were we supposed to do now?

"Well. This was illuminating, Jordan. I told you—they're paying him, not using him. Let's go," Otter said, rolling his eyes. Disappointed, we all rose.

"Paying me? *Ha,*" Hastings said. "They aren't paying me a dime!"

We stopped. "What?" I asked.

"SRS. They've never given me a penny."

"They're blackmailing you?" Walter said.

"Of course they're blackmailing me! I didn't want anything to do with them, but they'll ruin me. They'll take every dime I have! I won't be able to make my car payments. I won't be able to go to my house in Monaco. I won't be able to *keep* my house in Monaco! They'll destroy my *life!*" Hastings said, his face turning bright red as he got louder and louder.

"How are they blackmailing you? Maybe we can fix it," I said, ignoring the fact that losing a vacation house had worked this man into hysterics. "You had an affair? You . . . got arrested? Stole from the bank?"

"No, no, no," Hastings said mournfully. "Worse."

"Tell us," Kennedy said. "What's the worst that could happen? You're already being blackmailed."

Hastings considered this for a moment and sighed heavily. He stood up slowly, then walked out of the room.

"Uh, should we follow him?" Walter asked. I nodded, and we all sprang after him. Hastings led us through the kitchen, down some stairs, and to a little enclosed patio. He pointed to a bright-orange cushion on the ground.

"*That's* how they're blackmailing me," he said.

"They know about your . . . strange taste in beanbags?" Ben asked.

Hastings looked horrified. "That's not a beanbag! It's a dog! An extremely rare red-gold Tibetan mastiff!"

"A *dog*?" Kennedy squealed, and before anyone could stop her, she'd dropped to her knees and was crawling toward the cushion—er, the dog—with a hand extended, making kissing noises.

"This is International Supreme Grand Champion Her Lady's Most Gracious Reply," Hastings said. When Hastings said the dog's name, it lifted its head tiredly. It had giant droopy lips and eyes, and a mane like a lion's. It had to weigh three times what Kennedy weighed, at least. The dog leaned forward and stuck its nose into Kennedy's outstretched hand, sniffing her palm. It didn't get up, but its tail did begin to thump against the floor.

"She likes me! I like you too, International Supreme Grand . . . What was the rest of her name?" Kennedy said, glowing.

"Just call her Annabelle. The long name is just for show," Hastings said. Annabelle, apparently satisfied by the smell of Kennedy's hand, rolled over slightly, begging in the laziest way possible for her stomach to be rubbed.

"They're threatening your *dog*? That's evil, even for SRS," I said, shaking my head.

"No, no. They know the truth about my dog," Hastings said. He took a deep breath and then said, "I make my living off Annabelle. The bank doesn't pay much, but Annabelle's puppies bring in a half million per."

My jaw dropped. "A half million dollars for a puppy?"

"For a Tibetan mastiff puppy!" Hastings said indignantly. "It's the rarest dog in the world!"

"You have all this," Otter said, gesturing to the grandiose house, "from breeding *that* dog? The one that literally hasn't moved since we got here. That dog."

"She moved! She rolled over!" Kennedy said defensively.

Hastings went on quickly, "Well, no—I inherited the house—and Annabelle—from my grandmother when she passed. The old lady wouldn't leave me a dime of actual *money*. So I got a whole bunch of *stuff*—this house, some art that I sold, Annabelle . . . I was supposed to get more.

There was a set of jewel-encrusted books that I could've sold for millions and millions and lived off for the rest of my life, but those were stolen just before she died. So I live off Annabelle now. Without her, I'd lose everything. But SRS knows . . . Well . . . They know . . ." Hastings turned deep red and stared at the ground. His face contorted a bit, like he might cry. He then whispered something under his breath.

"What'd he say?" Walter asked me. I shrugged.

Hastings whispered again, a bit louder, "Theynosheez-nodapoorbed."

"What?" Ben asked.

Hastings threw his arms in the air. "They know she's not a purebred! My Annabelle is a lie! Her great-great-great-great-grandfather wasn't a Tibetan mastiff—he was a golden retriever!"

Then Hastings slumped down into a patio chair and buried his head in his hands. Otter regarded him like he was something old from the back of the refrigerator. Walter looked confused. Kennedy and Clatterbuck, who was now also patting Annabelle, didn't seem to think her scandalous grandfather dog did anything to lessen her charm.

"So . . . they're threatening to tell the world that Annabelle isn't a purebred. That's how they're making you handle their money for them," I said slowly.

Hastings nodded from behind his hands. "You see? There's nothing I can do. I have to help them. They'll ruin me," he mumbled into his fingers. "This is all my grandmother's fault, you know. *Make your way in the world,* she said. *Don't plan on living off my inheritance,* she said. *Get a job, you deadbeat,* she said. Then she gave all the money away and left me with *heirlooms,* and now there's nothing left to *sell,* and so all I've got is this *dog,* and now my house is full of *spies.*"

"Well, give us a chance to figure out how to get you out of all *this,*" Kennedy said, matching his tone. "We're good at *this.* We're professional spies, after all."

Otter snorted. I didn't say anything, but I sort of agreed with Otter.

Beatrix piped up, "She's right! They got me out of SRS headquarters, along with about a dozen other kids SRS kidnapped. So they can definitely figure out a way to get you out of being blackmailed."

"You can't make her a purebred, though. I have the papers forged, but if SRS even started a *rumor,* everyone would want a genetic test done. They'd see the golden retriever in her past." Hastings sniffed hopelessly.

"We'll think of something," I said, though he had a point. "And if we do this for you, Mr. Hastings, will you tell *us* which accounts SRS's money is in?"

Hastings nodded. "Sure. But there's no point. There's nothing you can do."

"Give us a chance. Like my sister said"—I took a breath, like saying it aloud might make it more true—"we're professionals."

CHAPTER SIX

"I'm just saying, the man has a job and a fancy house. Doesn't seem very noble to help a rich man *stay rich*," Ben said. Beatrix nodded in agreement.

He had a point—Hastings wasn't the most sympathetic of SRS victims. Still, I said, "Think big picture. We're not helping Markus Hastings—we're helping The League. We're helping everyone SRS hurts with that money."

We were spread out around the kitchen table again, brainstorming ways we could keep Annabelle's secret a secret. So far we had:

1. Fake a DNA test for Annabelle

(We could fake *her* test, but a decent lab would likely run an independent control *before* Annabelle's, and we couldn't fake that one so easily.)

2. Switch Annabelle out with a *real* red-gold Tibetan mastiff

(Nope—Annabelle was the only one in the world. In fact, the gold was probably "rare" because it was coming from her golden retriever roots.)

3. Clatterbuck goes in disguise as a dog-show judge

(There was no point to the costume, really; I think Clatterbuck just wanted to go somewhere in disguise, so he suggested this.)

"Maybe . . . maybe we're thinking about this the wrong way," Ben said. We looked to him. "See, sometimes when I'm inventing something, I get too fixated on what I want the end machine to *be* instead of what I want it to *do*. Like, wanting a woodcutting machine to *be* an ax-robot rather than *do* woodcutting."

"Is *that* what that is in the cafeteria closet? The thing with the ax?" Otter asked, horrified. "It can *move*?"

"It's fine, it's fine—I removed the motion-activation sensor," Ben said, waving Otter off. He continued, "So maybe, instead of trying to fix Annabelle, we need to think about fixing Hastings. The *real* problem is that he'll be ruined if Annabelle is outed. So we actually just need to find another way for him to make money."

"What about the books?" Clatterbuck suggested. "Didn't he say some fancy books were stolen? Gold or something?"

"Jewel-encrusted," Otter said. "We could find the books. He could sell them, live off *that*. He wouldn't need Annabelle anymore."

"Poor Annabelle!" Kennedy cried. Clatterbuck nodded and patted her shoulder.

"All right. So. We find the jeweled books. We get them back to Hastings. He gets us SRS's funding. We go home," I said, ticking the tasks off on my fingers.

Otter looked skeptical. "Jeweled books—there are a thousand different people who might want those. Book collectors. Jewel thieves. Art lovers. Everyone from the high-end criminal to some small-time thief looking to make a quick buck. SRS themselves might have taken them, actually, as leverage."

"So you're saying it's impossible?" Beatrix asked, crestfallen.

"I'm saying this is *not* a long-term mission. We can't stay in Switzerland for ages. Not only would SRS figure us out, but we can't afford it. We need a backup plan."

"Maybe Annabelle could do something else to earn Hastings some money," Kennedy suggested. "You know, like be one of those Saint Bernards that carries hot chocolate to lost hikers."

"That's just a myth. They never did that," I said, shaking my head.

"Well, then she could be the first," Kennedy said, and stuck her tongue out at me. "Just because she wasn't born some fancy-pants perfect Tibetan mastiff doesn't mean she can't still be a good dog."

I sighed, but I sort of understood what Kennedy meant. I wasn't born the perfect spy, after all. It wasn't Annabelle's fault her great-great-whatever was a golden retriever any more than it was my fault that I somehow inherited my great-aunt's arm flab.

"All right, all right—you teach Annabelle to do something useful," I said.

"I'll help! I once trained a dog to growl on command!" Clatterbuck said, nodding at Kennedy.

"Really?" Otter asked.

"Well, he growled whenever he saw me. Does that count?" Clatterbuck said. Now we *all* sighed. Unbelievably, this trip seemed a lot simpler when we were just breaking into a few hypersecure bank vaults.

"It can't hurt to *ask* Hastings when the books were stolen. Maybe we can figure it out. If we can't, we'll find another way," I said, shaking my head.

Otter glanced at me so fast, the others missed it. I knew what he was thinking though: *we* could threaten to out Annabelle's true heritage if Hastings didn't give us the account numbers. Obviously, it was a persuasive threat, since it worked for SRS. It would be quick. Tidy. Simple.

I shook my head at him almost imperceptibly. No, we couldn't—we couldn't do things like SRS. We were the good guys, after all. Still, years and years of SRS schooling made that solution so very tempting. How was SRS still in my head, even though I knew what they really were? Even though they'd lied to me for my entire life?

Sometimes, no matter how far I got from SRS, it felt like they were always right behind me.

Just in case we ever *did* get around to robbing the bank, we'd still need a way to get everything out from the vaults. Ben began drafting that evening, after we described the thickness of the bank carpet and the number of door-jambs in the lobby to him in detail. Beatrix was helping while Otter explained exactly how many steps it was from the front door to the wall of bankers' desks. There were twenty-three; I knew not because he'd told me, but because I'd counted them out as well. It's a spy thing.

Meanwhile, Clatterbuck was looking up helicopter tours of Geneva. ("Come on, when else will we all be in Geneva? It'll be fun!") Walter had gone for a walk, I guessed to see the ponies, since the last time I saw him he was walking toward the barn. I found Kennedy sitting in the bedroom she was sharing with Beatrix, flipping through a newspaper.

"Are you reading that?" I asked, surprised. She'd already taken German at SRS, but the paper was written in French, which she wouldn't learn till she was eleven.

"I'm trying," she said, sighing. She dropped the paper and slumped back on her bed, her red hair fanning out around her. Her side of the room was already ransacked— her suitcase was spilling pink and purple clothes onto the floor, and her sheets were in knots. Kennedy kicked the newspaper to the ground, where I suspected it would stay until we left.

I walked over and picked up the top piece of paper. "What did you want to read? I can translate it for you, maybe."

Kennedy gave me a hesitant look. "The classifieds."

I stopped and looked at her, then nodded. "I already checked this morning. But I'll go through them again, just in case."

I found the classifieds and scanned through them. Houses, cars, babysitters needed, weird personals from guys I definitely wouldn't call if I were a Swiss lady. Jobs. Apartments.

But I didn't see anything like what Kennedy was looking for—what we were *both* looking for every day: a secret message from our parents.

Kennedy and I hadn't seen Mom and Dad for months, since they left one morning to go on a mission for SRS and never returned. Last we'd heard from them was via a message hidden in the Castlebury classifieds, a message that led to a voice mail that explained how they couldn't come back just yet, because it wasn't safe. But that was it. No phone calls. No mail. No secret notes.

"There's nothing," I told Kennedy, setting the paper down. Kennedy nodded, pulling her feet up under her in a show of flexibility that made my knees hurt, but that she didn't even notice. She rocked back and forth for a second and then exhaled.

"You think they're okay, don't you, Hale?"

"Of course!" I said, furrowing my brow. "Of course I do. It's just not safe, like they said in the last message. But I bet they're keeping tabs on us. I bet they know we're in Switzerland."

"You think they'll send you something for your birthday?" Kennedy asked, her eyes lighting up.

I forced a smile. To be honest, I was trying really, really hard not to think about the fact that my parents wouldn't be around for my birthday. I hadn't reminded anyone that it was coming up in a few weeks, even.

"Maybe they will," I said, but I tried not to sound excited—I didn't want to get Kennedy's hopes up. It was just a birthday, anyway. I was going to be thirteen—that's too old to make a big deal out of the day you were born, right? And it's not like they could make me confetti pancakes like they used to back at SRS or sneak me out of Basic Parkour early to go to the little movie theater in Castlebury. My parents were too busy being heroes to worry about stuff like that these days. They were probably too busy to even *remember* my birthday, really.

I stooped and collected the newspaper, balling it up. "I'm going to bed, hopefully before Ben gets there. He snores. Does Beatrix?"

"No, but she does talk to her Right Hand in her sleep sometimes," Kennedy said thoughtfully.

"Lucky," I said, and left the room as Kennedy arranged a few stuffed animals along the top of her bed. I didn't even realize she'd packed them, but when I noticed them, I noticed that she'd also brought her own pink leopard-print blanket and a stack of coloring books.

Kennedy was always Kennedy—always neon and loud and sparkly. At SRS, at The League, even here in Geneva. I went back to my own room, where Ben had a thousand inventing things laid out on the spare bunk. I climbed up to look at Walter's bunk, above mine, and saw that he'd brought his own pillow and that stuffed frog (which was looking really worn-out these days).

And then I looked at my bed, which, like my room back at The League, was plain. There was nothing.

Because outside of SRS, I was nothing.

CHAPTER SEVEN

"Mr. Hastings, we'd like to help you find the jeweled books that were stolen," I said the next morning from the banker's front stoop.

"Huh? You mean the Runanko books?" he said faintly. He looked rather disappointed—like he'd hoped we were just a dream.

"If those are the ones that got stolen, yes. We'll help you get your Runanko books back, and it won't matter if your dog's a fraud," Otter responded.

Hastings's eyebrows lifted a bit as he shut the door. "I . . . Sure. I suppose. I mean, the police couldn't help recover them, but—"

"Let's talk about the theft with Beatrix and Ben so they can make notes," I said, and started into the house.

"Those kids?" Hastings said, looking behind me.

"That's our tech team," Otter said, his voice a combination of defeat and defense. It was hard not to be defensive about Beatrix and Ben. The SRS tech team was good, but they probably couldn't create a laser gun out of toilet paper rolls and disposable cameras.

Hastings shrugged and led us into the house. Clatterbuck and Kennedy rushed forward to find Annabelle, while Beatrix and Ben immediately began to set up their equipment in the living room. They removed a few books and plants off a wide coffee table and were buzzing around it, connecting things here, moving things there, unplugging lamps to plug in power cables. Beatrix looked up at me and then stuck her Right Hand into a port. The system sprang to life, far louder than any modern laptop but probably a thousand times more efficient.

Hastings sat down on the leather couch, leaving Otter and me to pull two elaborately embroidered wingback chairs up to the table. Like the other rooms of the house we'd seen, this one reeked of money—marble busts and oil paintings and furniture with fancy little gold bits. There were giant windows along the back wall, but even the sunlight couldn't compete with the dark burgundy rugs and heavy wood paneling. I felt sort of like we were in an old-fashioned movie, the kind with fox hunts and visits from the queen.

"Shall I . . . get the investigators' findings? My grandmother was utterly destroyed when they were stolen—she hired a private investigator and everything . . . ," Hastings said, staring at Beatrix's Right Hand. She was currently using it to open and control a half dozen windows on the various computer screens.

"Not yet—let's just start from the beginning. Tell me *when* the Runanko books were stolen, first off," I said.

"Almost twenty years ago."

Otter and I deflated at nearly the same moment. A twenty-year-old crime? This was already looking grim. Nonetheless, Beatrix nodded at Hastings and then typed something into her Right Hand. The computers lit up, flashing newspapers and memos and flight information from twenty years ago.

"Do you remember the day?" Beatrix asked. "We can narrow it down."

Hastings nodded. "It was a few days after my twelfth birthday party, which is February seventeenth—so, between then and perhaps the twenty-first?"

Beatrix typed in a bit more.

"Don't watch them, Mr. Hastings," I said, drawing his attention back. I'd learned in Basic Interrogation class back at SRS that memories are tricky things. People like to think memories are like videotape, where you can just rewind and see a scene exactly as it was. Unfortunately, they're more like clouds—you think you know what you see, but then something shifts, and suddenly it's a whole different image. I worried that Hastings might see something on

Beatrix's screens that would alter the way he told his story. Then again, he'd likely been questioned about the theft so many times that his memory was already junked up . . .

Ugh. Twenty years!

"Right," Hastings answered. "Well. My grandmother was still alive, of course. They were her books, something my grandfather had given her for her birthday. They were kept downstairs in the library along with our original Picasso and this weird Fabergé egg being pulled in a wagon by an angel. Russians. Strange taste, right?" We didn't react, so he kept going. "Anyway, the books just disappeared one day."

He stopped.

"That's it?" I asked.

Hastings nodded. "They just vanished. Look, it may seem easy to break into this house *now*, since I can't afford to pay a staff, but back in the day we had security. And there were all sorts of fancy weight-related alarms that should have gone off if the books were lifted, but they didn't. Whoever came in got them and got out without us even noticing."

"Okay . . . you said you had a birthday party. Do you remember who came?" I asked. From somewhere farther inside the house, I heard Kennedy and Clatterbuck calling Annabelle's name over and over. At first I thought they had lost her and were trying to get her to return, but then I heard Kennedy adding "Come on! Get up! You can do it!" and realized no, they were just trying to make her *move*. While I listened, Hastings ticked off the guest list on his fingers.

"Let's see—the upcountry Deans, Alabasters, the St. Claire sisters—I remember because they made fun of me for having a clown at my party when I was twelve years old—the Stonemans, Princess Ygritte—"

"A princess?" Beatrix looked up, impressed.

"Only of a little principality," Hastings said, rolling his eyes. "Though if you ask her, I'm sure she'd give you some long boring history about—"

"Any of them interested in the books?" Otter cut him off.

"All rich people want pretty things," Hastings said, shrugging.

"What about household staff? Those security guys you mentioned?" I asked.

Hastings shook his head. "The police cleared them all. But I can get you the names."

Beatrix and Ben had been hurriedly entering all the information—cross-referencing the family names Hastings had thrown out with arrest records, searching auction listings. I met Beatrix's eyes; she gave me a "nope" sort of look and then went back to typing.

Hastings led us downstairs to show us the room the books were stolen out of. The walls were entirely bare, save for a giant emblem of the Geneva Country Club, which hung above the fireplace. Lights shone down from the ceiling at empty platforms and vacant picture hooks. No wonder Annabelle was so valuable to him—from the looks of things, there was nothing left to sell.

"What did they look like, exactly?" I asked.

"There are three of them. Emeralds on one, rubies on another, sapphires on the last one. The pages are this sort of see-through material—vellum, I think it's called—and they're all hand painted. My understanding was that they were as valuable for their artistic value as for their jewels. Jeweled manuscripts are already rare, but that particular set is sort of famous. The *Mona Lisa* of jeweled books."

"And they've never appeared on the black market as far as you know?" Otter said, frowning.

"Not a trace. Whoever has them must be holding on to them, I guess the same way Grandma Hastings did. You know, if she'd just left me a decent inheritance, these stupid old books wouldn't even be an issue. But nooooo. She didn't leave me a dime—"

"She left you with a mansion and a million-dollar dog," Otter said flatly.

"Sure, sure. A million-dollar dog and a *day job* at the stupid bank my family started a billion years ago," Hastings said, waving his hand in the air. "I'm not even an upper-level manager, you know! They say I have to get a stupid degree for that. But anyway, you really think you can find them?" Hastings asked as he led us upstairs. "I'd do anything to get them back. They're worth even more now."

I tried to scowl at him—I could practically see him calculating how much money he'd make selling his grandmother's prized possession.

"It won't be easy. But we'll try," I said. The truth was, this was getting more and more hopeless. Those books could have been divided up. They could have been broken down, the jeweled covers split into a thousand pieces and sold separately.

On the way back upstairs, we crossed paths with Kennedy and Clatterbuck, as well as Annabelle, who was walking behind them so slowly that if you'd told me she was sleepwalking, I would've believed you.

"She's moving?" Hastings said, looking alarmed. "She never moves."

Annabelle looked up at him with droopy, tired eyes, then back at Kennedy. Her tail began to wag a bit. Hastings looked offended, while Kennedy looked delighted.

"That's right! Good girl!" Kennedy cried, and fed her a piece of a toaster waffle.

"What are you—she's a show dog! She can't have waffles. Go to the kitchen—there are some t-r-e-a-t-s in the silver canister," Hastings said grouchily.

"We tried those. She doesn't like them," Kennedy said pointedly, like this was something Hastings should have known (and really, he should have). "Come on, Annabelle, let's go find a toy."

Kennedy's enthusiasm seemed to be rubbing off on the dog, because Annabelle trotted after her—actually *trotted*.

Hastings looked like he was worried about her, what with all that movement.

"Any luck with the books?" Clatterbuck interrupted Hastings's alarm.

"We're getting there," I lied. "Beatrix and Ben are putting together all the information from earlier. Mr. Hastings, why don't you go see if there's anything they've missed while the three of us talk this through?" I suggested. Hastings shrugged and walked off. The hair covering his bald spot flapped a bit as he went by the air-conditioning vent. Once he was out of sight, Otter and I sighed in unison.

"That bad?" Clatterbuck asked.

"There's no point. There was only one solid team of art thieves working Europe twenty years ago, only one team that took things like books and furniture and statues instead of focusing on paintings, like most thieves."

"Who?" Clatterbuck asked.

Otter laughed meanly and then looked at me. "Your parents, Jordan."

CHAPTER EIGHT

My parents were not art thieves.

They just weren't. They were heroes, and it wasn't like you could just rob a little old lady of some fancy books and *not* know that was a decidedly unheroic thing to do.

"SRS did a lot of bad things, Jordan, and your parents were SRS agents. Art theft was their *thing* actually—that's how they got partnered up," Otter said smugly on the way back to the *poney* farm.

"Your theory doesn't make sense even if my parents *were* thieves. If SRS had the books, they could just promise to return them to Hastings to blackmail him. They wouldn't need to bring Annabelle into it at all. There are a dozen way more likely scenarios, and probably thousands of art thieves in the world."

Otter snorted. "Sure. And most of them work for SRS."

No one else weighed in, not even after we got back to the farmhouse—I wasn't sure if this was because they believed me, because they believed Otter, or because they just didn't want to get in the middle of it. Instead we sat down at the kitchen table and sorted through the lists of birthday party attendees, Hastings's family friends, and household staff. By dinner I'd memorized nearly all of them.

"I just don't see any history that makes me think these people would steal," Beatrix said for the thousandth time, shaking her head as she looked at photos of the party attendees. She'd easily grabbed them off the Internet—as it turns out, famous people get their pictures taken a lot.

"The friends, at least, are superrich. They can probably make a crime disappear," I said. "Especially if they weren't stealing the art to sell, but just to keep. There was some guy who stole two hundred paintings once just because he was trying to put together a personal collection."

"Right!" Kennedy said brightly—she hadn't been able to contribute much, and seemed pumped to know something. "He got caught, and his mom tore them all up to try and hide the evidence!"

Ben looked horrified. "Really? Two hundred paintings? I don't know what I'd do if someone tore up all my blueprints. How do you two know all that?"

My voice hitched, so Kennedy wound up beating me to the punch. "Our parents told us the story."

And then we all fell silent again, because by this point, everyone had heard Otter's theory about my parents' thieving past. No one believed it, of course—at least, I hoped no one did.

"They knew a lot about a lot of stuff," I said swiftly. "It doesn't mean anything. Agent Otter never much liked my parents. I think he's just trying to blame them, and we'll end up wasting time following that, got it? Let's focus."

Kennedy took a big breath and then looked around the room. "I think Hale's right. Let's go through the list and start clearing people who were in the house twenty years ago."

Walter clapped his hands. "All right, yeah. I trust you, Hale. You got us this far, right?"

I tapped the table, trying to hype myself back up. "Okay, so—tomorrow. Kennedy, why don't you visit the people who used to work in the house? Just nose around, get some preliminary information. Ben, want to go with her?"

Ben whooped. "Yes! It'll be perfect for me to test out the BEN-ray gun. It's sort of an X-ray gun. It'll send a digital X-ray photo to Beatrix's Right Hand. If we're able to get into anyone's house, we can X-ray safes or secret rooms to get a look inside. Plus I think I've gotten the misfires down to just one every ten shots, really."

"Good. Be careful. With the BEN-ray gun, I mean," I said. Ben looked a little affronted but then nodded reluctantly. Kennedy gave me a thumbs-up and a grin.

"And then, Beatrix—I'll need you to run mission control from here for me and Walter. We have all the comm devices here, right?"

"Yep, Ben and I packed them all," Beatrix said.

"All right. We need those, and we need suits or something."

"Suits? Are we going on a fancy date?" Walter asked, leaning his chair onto its legs. He balanced there for a moment and then tipped back to the floor.

"We're going to the Geneva Country Club," I said.

When Otter woke up the next morning, Kennedy and Ben were already on their way to visit the homes of a few retired Hastings employees—a maid or two, and the butler. Beatrix had rerouted a dry-cleaning delivery to the *poney* farm, so Walter and I had suits on the way, and she'd also secured us cover identities—we were going in as the sons of some sort of oil baron. By the time Clatterbuck finished cleaning up the waffles he'd made everyone for breakfast, Walter and I had pinned and tweaked the suits so they looked passable.

"Not a chance," Otter said when we came downstairs.

"What? Why not?" Walter said, turning in a circle.

"You look acceptable, Quaddlebaum," Otter told Walter. "But, Jordan, that suit doesn't and never has fit you."

"Obviously, but—"

"A rich person is going to know the difference between a tailored suit and something off-the-rack. And the people at the Geneva Country Club are rich. You need a different outfit," Otter said. I wanted to scowl at him, but then I got a glimpse of myself in the mirror. Otter was right. Walter's suit looked off-the-rack. I, however, looked like someone had melted a suit onto me. The sleeves were too long, the neck was too small, and the pants went around my waist all right but then bunched up under my butt. I thought about the seamstress at SRS, Ms. Elma. Mean as she was, I wished she were here. She'd have the thing fitting perfectly in less than a quarter hour.

And then I scowled at *myself*, because there I was again, wishing for SRS.

"Let me think," Otter said. Behind him, Clatterbuck hopped up and down on his toes. He looked like he might burst. Otter turned to look at him. "Don't tell me—you've got suits in your suitcase of disguises? Or wait, no—tuxedos. Ball gowns?" Otter sounded oddly hopeful.

"No—well, yes, but they'll fit only me. But I do know where I can find something for Hale and Walter. Hang on," Clatterbuck said eagerly, and took off through the house. Curiosity got to me, Walter, and Otter; we followed

Clatterbuck, who stopped in the center of the hallway and yanked on a cord, revealing attic stairs. We climbed up after him into a surprisingly tidy attic. There were boxes everywhere, but they were neatly labeled, and plastic sheets protected what little furniture was there. Clatterbuck threw open the lid of a nearby trunk, the old-fashioned kind with an arched top.

"I checked the whole place for bugs the first day, and I saw these," he explained as he rooted around in the trunk, his body blocking our view.

"Really?" Otter asked, impressed. I'll admit it—I think we all sometimes forgot that, strange as he was, Clatterbuck had been a League agent once. I felt smug on Clatterbuck's behalf, and I grinned at Otter's surprised expression.

"Here, here," Clatterbuck said, finally rising from the trunk. He was holding . . . some folded khaki pants.

"Huh?" Walter asked.

"The style hasn't changed in . . . well. In forever, basically. So they won't even look out of date!" Clatterbuck said excitedly.

"Khaki pants?" I asked.

Clatterbuck laughed. "No!" He let one pair of pants unfold and then held them up for us to see. "It's a riding habit. This farm only does breeding now, but before the owners retired, they were a show stable. This is what you wear to ride a horse in a fancy show."

I grinned. "Or what we'd wear if we'd just finished riding horses at a fancy country club?"

"Exactly!" Clatterbuck says, pleased. "And maybe I can find some hats! And a riding crop! And maybe we can even borrow one of the horses—"

I patted Clatterbuck's shoulder. "I think the clothes will be plenty."

It took a few changes before Walter and I found habits that fit. Well, "fit" is a word I'm using very, very loosely.

Walter, given the fact that every day the guy practically grew another inch, looked like an honest-to-goodness Olympian. I mean, seriously—he could have walked right out and jumped on a horse and won the gold medal for the Republic of Muscle Tone. I, on the other hand, looked like a sausage being strangled. My legs barely fit into the spandex-y pants. They were a little too long, which only made me look shorter. The white shirt was decent enough, but when I tucked it in, my body kind of looked like a mushroom cloud of smoke erupting from the pants.

You'd think this kind of thing wouldn't bother me as much anymore, now that I wasn't surrounded by classmates making fun of me. You'd be wrong.

But we had work to do, so I sighed, gave Walter a *yeah, I know it's bad* look, and the two of us went on our way.

CHAPTER NINE

The Geneva Country Club was right on the edge of Lake Geneva, the lake the city was named after. It had a spectacular view of the snowcapped mountains and a billion old trees with gnarled branches thicker than my body. It also had a very big gate out front, with a very big security guard. He waved people in fancy cars through one at a time, smiling and greeting them in a variety of languages—it was pretty impressive.

"Excusez-moi, monsieurs!" the guard said, stepping in front of us. *"Peux-je vous aidez?"* Can I help you?

I smiled at him brightly and answered in French, but I let my voice take on a bit of a British accent, since the Kessel brothers were at school in England. "Hello—Sven, yes? We're here with our father, Monsieur Theodore Kessel."

"He's an oil baron!" Walter said cheerily. I did my best not to glare.

"Monsieur Kessel?" the guard said, eyeing Walter suspiciously. "But he went in ages ago. Why weren't you with him?"

I looked at Walter and folded my arms. "That would be because of my *dear* brother here, and his big mouth. Victor complained about father not sending any decent horses with us to school. Then they got in an argument. Then Father said that if we were going to be so unappreciative, perhaps it'd do us well to learn the value of hard work. And then—well, let me summarize it for you: he threw us out of the limo a kilometer back. I think my brother's a little dizzy from all the walking here," I said, lowering my voice at the end.

Sven laughed broadly and gave Walter a pitying look. He dropped his voice a bit. "Well, that was a bold thing for him to say, seeing as how your father inherited his fortune, no? But let's leave that between us." He winked. "All right, all right—go on in, gentlemen. *Passez un bon après-midi!*"

I grinned at him, and Walter and I hustled in. Walter looked like his heart rate was just now slowing—the whole bit about getting thrown out of the limo was off book, and it'd rattled him. What was crazy about Walter was that he *had* all the skills to be an amazing spy. It was just that he always freaked out and worried he *didn't*, and that wrecked him.

"You okay?" I asked him.

"Yeah. Yeah," he said. "Sorry. I just haven't done any real fieldwork in . . . well. Since you and I were on that mission to the sports school for SRS."

We walked toward the country club's main building, sidestepping golf carts and the occasional horseback rider—who were *indeed* wearing the exact same clothes Walter and I were. We stuck our chests out, like the proud sons-of-a-rich-guy we were, looking down only to check that our nails were clean.

The main building looked something like a castle—in fact, I think it used to actually *be* a castle. It was solid stone, with large, arched wood doors and honest-to-goodness turrets at the tops, which were dotted with white and red flags. Behind flower-covered windows, I could see giant leather sofas and ladies wearing thick pearl necklaces. Black cars were delivering a constant stream of fabulously dressed people to the wood doors, where a butler wearing white gloves bowed a bit and ushered the visitors inside. For a moment I worried that the butler would question us like the guard had, but no—when we walked up, he merely tipped his head to us, smiled, and held the door. We were in.

Now we just needed to find some kids our age. Here was what I figured—the books were likely stolen by one of the adults at Hastings's birthday party. Those adults were in their sixties now. And their kids—the ones who were Hastings's age—were in their thirties and forties. But *their* kids would be around my age and, if I had to guess, didn't even know those fancy jeweled books in their family castle were stolen. Because, come on—what kind of parent would tell his children that dear old mom and dad were thieves?

We found a handful of kids our age down by the pool. There were only about six or seven total—hanging out at your parents' country club probably wasn't the most popular of activities—but together they looked like a *collection*. These kids all looked like variations on the same thing—the same way stamps or coins or different types of cats are all variations on the same thing. They all had the same bored expression. They all had on designer sunglasses. Almost all were tapping away on phones or tablets or laptops. The handful that wasn't was lying on towels, looking bored, or reapplying lip gloss (both the boys *and* the girls).

Two girls looked up as we walked into the pool area. Their eyes glanced off me immediately; when they saw Walter, they tipped their sunglasses down their noses and grinned.

I ducked my head so no one would see me talking into my comm. "Beatrix, we've got two girls—thirteenish. One brown hair, one blond hair. Blonde has a Band-Aid on her arm, the sort you'd get after you get a shot—"

"Okay, okay, hang on . . ." Beatrix typed frantically back at the *poney* farm. "Perfect—the blonde is Aria

Stoneman—she's the youngest of the Stoneman family, and they were at Hastings's party. Pulling up records now . . . Looks like Aria just got inoculations for a glamping trip to Africa."

"Glamping?" Walter muttered.

"Glamour camping. It's like camping, only the tent is a five-star tent with running water and a Jacuzzi."

"Wow. Okay, *glamping*. Got it," I said, which was a lie. I most certainly did not have this. We approached.

"Hey," I said. Walter grinned at me, as if to say, *Strong start!*

"Hi," Aria said simply, though not unkindly. "You're new."

I laughed nervously. "Yeah—to this club, anyway. I'm George. This is Ringo." Walter frowned at his new fake name—but it wasn't like we could have been Albert and Victor Kessel to *these* people. They probably knew the real Kessel brothers, or at least, would know that we weren't them.

Beatrix tittered in my ear. "Ringo?"

Aria smiled. Her teeth were perfectly straight. "Parents have a thing for the Beatles, huh? My name's Aria. Were you two out riding?"

I laughed a little. "Yeah. Didn't think to bring a change of clothes, and now we're stuck here till Dad finishes his golf game."

"I know the feeling," Aria said. "My mom's always, *Aria, they have a pool! It'll be fun!* And then I'm stuck here for hours and hours and hours. Like I don't have anything better to do than sit at her country club—"

"Glamping. I know what glamping is," Walter interrupted. I lifted my eyebrows at him. *Slick, Walter. Slick.*

"Uh . . . cool," Aria said, then looked back to her book.

Walter gave me an apologetic look; I tried not to sigh too heavily at him. I turned my head to give Beatrix physical descriptions as often as I could, and eventually, she'd helped me pinpoint Jeffery Alabaster and Archimedes St. Claire in addition to Aria. Three grandchildren of our potential art thieves.

Those were the kids we *had* to get talking.

I sat down on a pool chair close to Archimedes St. Claire; a waiter on the other side of the pool whisked over a glass of water so fast, it made me jump. I thanked him and tried to find my way back to a conversation—it'd mostly fizzled, with nearly everyone returning to their phones or drinks or bored stares.

"So, what would you be doing if you weren't here, then?" I asked Aria.

Aria frowned. "I don't know. Something else."

"Movies! People go to movies," Walter said.

I was beginning to wish I'd sent *Walter* to the movies.

Aria looked bemused this time. "Sure. I could go to the movies, I guess. Or . . ." She put her book down and looked suddenly discouraged. "I don't know, actually. I've just always had to come to the country club or go on their yacht or to the house in Paris."

"Or that fancy hotel in Australia," Archimedes chimed in.

"Yeah. That. But I bet I could find something to do," Aria said wistfully.

I nodded. "I get it. Sometimes it feels like you just live in your parents' world, right?"

"Right," Aria and Archimedes said in unison.

The conversation drifted off a bit—I had to get them back on board, keep them talking, so I could steer us into discussing art and whether a set of fancy books might be tucked away in their basements. The easiest way to keep someone talking was to *give* them something. An offering, a trade, a token of trust—a gift, no matter how small, greased the wheels. But what could I give kids who had everything?

Exactly what they wanted: a way out of their parents' world.

I looked over at Walter, and said loudly, "Let's get out of here, man."

Walter frowned. "Huh?"

"Let's get out of here. I saw some golf carts out back by the trees. That's way better than sitting around by a pool. We could do this at home."

With my peripheral vision, I saw heads lift, eyes flit onto us. Walter spoke again, a little loud, a little too much like he was in a play, but it'd do. "All right. Yeah. The pool is lame!"

"So you're going to go play golf?" one of the collection kids—it was Archimedes—said from a few lawn chairs away. He looked skeptical.

I laughed. "No. We're going to steal a car. Well. A golf cart."

Now I really had everyone's attention. Aria closed her book; Jeffery put his phone down and sat up. The other collection kids leaned forward. I waited till they were all staring, all eager, to say, "Anyone wanna help?"

No one said anything.

I shrugged. "All right, fine. Stay here. Have a nice day, ladies and gentlemen."

"Wait!" Aria said, and jumped up. She grinned. "I wanna help. I mean, it's just a golf cart. We can't get in *that* much trouble, right?"

CHAPTER TEN

The others agreed with Aria ("I mean, even if we get caught, it won't be as bad as the time I burned down the guest wing . . .") and followed me and Walter outside. The golf carts were where I expected them to be, based on the traffic patterns I'd noticed out front, but there was a caddie standing at the front of each, his eyes glazed over with heat and general world-weariness.

"Beatrix—" I muttered into my comm.

"Please, Hale. As if I wasn't already doing it," she said, laughing. Another second, and suddenly the caddie's walkie-talkie crackled. A voice—Clatterbuck's voice—said, "We need all caddies out front. We have an emergency. Someone's golf clubs have . . . uh . . . exploded."

"*What?*" the caddie said just as I said the exact same thing to Beatrix.

"I told him to come up with a caddie emergency!" she said.

"I do not get paid enough to deal with exploding golf clubs," the caddie muttered in German and then ran toward the front of the building. I crossed the path as he rounded the stone wall; the others followed me, looking delighted and confused. I motioned for everyone to get into the golf carts that were on the shady side, where the trees would hide us from view of the restaurant's veranda.

I stopped at the first cart and swallowed. I'd read about doing this in Automotive Handling class at SRS but had never done it. Walter looked as anxious as the collection kids, which wasn't giving me much confidence—I'd been hoping he'd be able to help, if I forgot . . .

"I need your hair band," I said to Aria.

"Wait, what?" she said.

"It'll be great—trust me," I said, holding out my hand.

Aria looked at Archimedes, Jeffery, and the rest of the collection, and then reached up and pulled the rubber band out of her hair. I grinned the way I thought my dad would—he's the mischievous sort—then popped open the plastic cover behind the golf cart seat.

"So, there's this thing on golf carts—they call it the governor. It keeps you from being able to go really fast," I explained as I reached down into the engine. "But you can disable it with"—I withdrew my hands and looked up at everyone—"a well-placed hair band."

"So we can . . . go fast in a golf cart?" Archimedes said, sounding unimpressed.

"You'd rather go back to the pool?" Walter asked, folding his arms.

Archimedes shook his head emphatically and then turned to another one of the collection girls. "Give me your hair tie, Merry. Or wait, no—give it to *him*. You can take the mayor off this one too, right?" he asked, tapping the next golf cart in line.

I grinned. "The *governor*. And absolutely."

There were eight of us—me, Walter, Aria, Jeffery, Archimedes, and another three collection kids, so we packed in the carts four each. Archimedes was driving the second; he climbed in, gave me a tentative look, and then tapped the accelerator. The golf cart lunged forward— Archimedes braked and then grinned recklessly.

"This is going to be *awesome*," he said. "Let's go!"

Then he floored it; the cart tilted onto two wheels and nearly tipped, but then it shot forward like a bullet from a gun. Walter slid into the passenger seat of my golf cart; Aria and Jeffery leaped onto the back, clutching the edges of the roof.

"Go! They're getting away!" Aria squealed, pointing.

I smashed my foot onto the accelerator, and we jetted off. Aria and Jeffery howled from the backseat as we raced after Archimedes and the others. We broke out of the shade and onto the shockingly green golf course.

I glanced toward the main building; a few heads were turning, people looking up from wine and brandy to see what the shouting on the course was all about. Walter waved.

"That's my dad on the veranda! He's going to kill me!" Aria yelled, but she sounded thrilled about it.

Archimedes braked as he went down a hill—I didn't. We crested the hill with a bounce so hard, Walter's head hit the top of the golf cart, and for a second I thought Jeffery had fallen off entirely. But no—I heard him yelling out insults as we shot ahead of Archimedes, away from the golf cart and toward the equestrian trails—

"Turn right! *Right!*" Aria roared. "Or we'll have to go over the stream!"

I nailed the brakes and spun the steering wheel hard to the right so that the car slid into place—then shot off again. Archimedes was behind us, but he was getting farther and farther away. The wind was making my eyes water, and I could smell the golf cart's engine burning, the consequence of making a car meant to go five miles an hour top out at thirty. I pressed harder, and we careened over a small fallen log; I almost lost control, but they didn't teach SRS kids how to drive getaway cars in third grade for nothing. Walter and I seamlessly leaned to the left, rebalanced the car, and kept going.

"What are you doing? Why is it so loud?" Beatrix shouted in my ear.

"Golf cart race!" I shouted back, knowing Aria and Jeffery couldn't possibly hear anything over their own howling laughter.

"Oh. Carry on," Beatrix said. "Except know they just entered you guys into the security log—they're coming after you on . . . well. On golf carts."

Slow golf carts, I thought.

A crash ahead of us—it was Archimedes bounding out of the woods. There were leaves stuck in his—and his passengers'—hair, but they were all grinning wickedly. I slammed on the brakes, skidding to a stop inches from the other cart.

The collection went wild with laughter.

"Wow. We're in so much trouble." Archimedes celebrated, punching his fist into the air.

"Did you guys see us go over the hill? How much air did we get?" Jeffery asked.

"It was, like, three feet. At *least,*" one of the girls—Merry, right?—answered.

"I'm thinking five, personally," Walter joined in, high-fiving Archimedes. They jostled Walter and clapped their hands on his shoulders, and for a moment I felt left out—till they hauled me toward the center of the circle and did the same. I laughed, tried not to enjoy it—but wow, it was nice fitting in, being the hero for something as stupid as making a golf cart go faster.

"Security! Go, go!" Archimedes shouted, pointing through the trees. Cutting through the path of downed

weeds we'd created was a golf cart with a piddly little blue light on its top. The driver shouted at us in French and then jumped out.

The other four kids took off running and, to my relief, the officer followed them.

"Come on!" Aria said hurriedly. "They'll send someone else, I bet. I know where we can go." Then she took off into the trees so fast that I almost missed what direction she'd gone in. Luckily, Jeffery was familiar—we followed him, and eventually, the four of us emerged into a little picnic area that I supposed was meant for the horseback riders to relax in. There were umbrellas and tables and even a little water trough for horses.

"Wow," Aria said, slumping onto a chair. "That was fantastic. You guys are great."

Jeffery laughed and shoved her familiarly. "See if you're saying that once you're grounded forever. Aria's dad thinks she's like a statue or something. She might shatter at any moment."

"He's just afraid I'll wind up being one of those heiress party girls," Aria said, but she didn't sound very convincingly defensive. "Though he won't let me get a pet iguana, which I really, really want, and how nonheiress-party-girl is that? It's not like I'm asking for a little purse dog."

"You're weird. Iguanas are weird," Jeffery said.

"Your dad keeps a white tiger as a pet. At least the iguana won't eat me," Aria said, and stuck her tongue out.

I sat down, catching my breath. Sweat was making my white shirt nearly transparent, but there wasn't much to be done about that, so I tried to ignore it. *Come on, Hale, conversation, steer the conversation*—"So, that's it, though? You'll get grounded?"

"I'm sure. But then he'll go out of town on business and he won't know the difference anyhow. It's not so bad," she said, and grinned. "Besides, that was the most fun I've had all summer. Maybe I should turn to a life of crime, stealing golf carts. A criminal mastermind. Think I'd make a good thief?"

"Sure. That's just it—being ready to jump up and *do* something rather than overthink it is the key to being a mastermind or thief or spy—"

Whoa. What was I doing? These were marks, not friends. I was casing them for information, not having a real conversation. Even *if* Aria and the others were a lot more like me than I thought. We were all trapped in a world we didn't create or control or ask for—

No. Keep moving.

Thankfully, Aria asked at that exact moment, "What about you guys? What's the punishment? I mean, you've done this before, I'm guessing?"

Walter laughed. "Oh yeah. This isn't so bad. Probably get our phones taken away or something like that."

Finally—an in. I trod carefully; I couldn't mess this up.

I said, "Remember when we stole that Jet Ski and it ran out of gas on that little island? Man. I thought we'd have to find the Runanko books to make them forgive us for *that*."

Walter nodded. Jeffery lifted an eyebrow. "The Runanko books? What are those?"

I rolled my eyes, like even explaining it all irritated me. "My parents collect art, and they're forever looking for these fancy books. They're all covered in gemstones and . . . I dunno. They're fancy, I guess."

"Jeweled books?" Aria said, frowning. "Who would put jewels on books?" Before I could answer, Jeffery cut in—

"My parents are *so* not into art. Our house is all modern and white and plastic. It's gross," he said.

"Crossing the Alabaster family off the list, in that case," Beatrix said quietly in my ear.

"What about Archimedes?" I said, pretending to joke. "Should've seen if *his* family has them. We could've raced for them, and if we'd won, we'd be out of trouble for the rest of our lives."

"Ha—if his family had something like that, they'd sell it. I heard they're broke," Jeffery said haughtily.

"And there goes the St. Claire family," Beatrix said.

Aria gave Jeffery a disgusted look. "Seriously, Jeffery? Archie is our friend. Don't go around airing his family's dirty laundry."

Jeffery rolled his eyes. "What? These guys are our friends too."

"We don't even know their last names," Aria argued, and then the truth of what she'd just said seemed to occur to her. She turned to me and Walter. "What *are* your last names, George and Ringo?"

"Kessel," Walter said confidently.

"Oh! Wait—hang on. Kessel?" Aria said.

"I thought the Kessels were . . . Victor and . . . What was the other's name? They were here a few weeks ago. You guys . . ." Jeffery's eyes went wide. "You're totally *not* the Kessel brothers."

Walter looked like he might faint. I felt my stomach flip, but I kept my cool—I mean, these were two kids my age. I'd been interrogated by the SRS director just a few months ago. I could handle that—I could handle this. I just needed an excuse that *wouldn't* get these two worried about us.

I sighed. "All right, fine—we're not the Kessel brothers."

Aria looked stunned—impressed but stunned. "Who are you? Do your parents even belong here?"

"George and Ringo, remember?" I said, grinning. "And no, they don't—though they are art collectors. And they do like the Beatles. But no, they don't belong here—we just snuck in for fun."

"You snuck *into* the country club for *fun*?" Jeffery said, and now his eyes were a mixture of horrified and delighted. "And convinced us to steal a car with you?"

"You *are* criminal masterminds!" Aria said.

"We stole a golf cart, not the *Mona Lisa*," I reminded her. Through the trees, we heard voices—backup security, I guess. I looked over at Jeffery and Aria. We were almost out of time, and we still hadn't ruled out Aria's family. The voices were getting closer . . . It wasn't the end of the world to be caught by country club security, but our photos would almost definitely be taken, in that case, which was never a good idea—SRS had plenty of face-recognition software at their disposal, after all.

"What's your name, really?" Aria asked, crossing her arms. She looked . . . amused? Curious? Maybe a little angry? It was hard to pinpoint.

I sighed, held out my hands. "It's Michael Hendrickson. But everything else we said was true, I swear. So if you've got those Runanko books, now would be a good time to sell them to me, because we're so grounded forever when those security guys get here."

Aria frowned and looked at the woods and then back to where the security officers were making their way down to us. "I don't know what your book things are, but you won't need them."

"Why not?" Walter asked.

Aria smiled at us. "Because you were never here."

Walter cocked his head. "Huh?"

I grabbed his arm and looked over at Aria, then at Jeffery, who looked pretty overwhelmed by the last hour of his life. "Aria Stoneman: Criminal Mastermind. I think it *does* have a nice ring to it," I said, and then dragged Walter into the woods.

I heard Aria's laugh, bright and loud above the trees—"Call me if you decide to go on another adventure—hey, wait! How did you know my last name?"

But Walter and I were already out of sight.

CHAPTER ELEVEN

Beatrix sent Clatterbuck to pick us up. He arrived driving a taxi and wearing a woman's wig and bright-red lipstick. It was pretty much one of the most horrifying things I'd ever seen. Stan Clatterbuck made one ugly woman. It didn't help that the wig was too small; every time we went through a roundabout, he had to clutch it to keep it affixed to his head. By the time we got back to the *poney* farm, his lipstick was smudged, and a strip of false eyelashes was stuck to his hand.

"I bet Kennedy and Ben had more luck than we did," I said as the three of us made our way inside. As soon as we opened the door, though, I realized this wasn't the case—Kennedy, Beatrix, Ben, and Otter were gathered around the kitchen table, looking defeated.

"No luck?" I asked unnecessarily. They shook their heads. Kennedy looked especially apologetic, and I knew she thought she'd let me down. I pulled on one of her red pigtails as I joined them at the table and she smiled but still looked sad.

Ben said, "They don't have the books, Hale, and I don't think they *ever* had them. They had nice houses, but they didn't have I-stole-and-sold-priceless-jeweled-books houses."

I took a breath. "Okay, then, what about the names Hastings gave us that weren't at the country club? That princess, for example?"

"I ruled her out while you guys were gone," Beatrix said. "And the upcountry Deans too. They're broke, and Princess Ygritte is afraid of paper, so I can't imagine she stole some books. It's called *papyrophobia*. It's a real thing, I swear."

"Well. Who do we have left then?" I asked.

I regretted asking immediately. Everyone's eyes dropped to the floor—except Otter's. He gave me a serious look and said, "SRS. Specifically, your parents."

I yanked out one of the chairs and sat down; the riding pants rode up uncomfortably, but I ignored them. "We've already gone over this, Otter. My parents aren't thieves," I said, looking over at my sister. Kennedy nodded along sort of meekly and then pulled her knees up to her chest and yanked them under her shirt.

"Your parents were SRS agents. They were whatever SRS told them to be," Otter said, stepping toward me. He wasn't much taller than me, but since I was sitting, it gave him a chance to tower a bit. "Jordan, I entertained this *chase* for a day, but if we're going to continue this mission, it's time we get serious about it. The odds are SRS—and your parents—took the books."

"Serious? You think I'm not serious just because your idea is ridiculous?" I said, and I felt my heart bounce around my chest. I tried to douse it—letting Otter see he'd gotten to me wouldn't help anything.

Luckily, Walter cut in while I got my emotions back under control. He stepped between me and Otter, holding his hands up. "Wait, wait—we didn't just go on a *chase* today. It's good that we cleared the rest of the house guests and staff, Agent Otter—"

"*Director* Otter," Otter corrected.

"Uh, right, Director, whatever. Well, it's good we cleared the staff and the country club families." Walter turned to me now and gave me a long look. "But maybe . . . Hale, maybe we just *look* into the possibility that SRS stole the books."

"You're believing *Otter* over me now?" I said.

Otter threw his arms out. "Why would I lie about this? Your parents were art thieves! Beatrix, hack into SRS and show him the old mission logs—"

"Uh, they've really locked their system up, so—" Beatrix began, but I cut her off.

"Not everything in the world goes back to SRS! And not everything is my parents' fault, no matter how much you hate them!" I snapped, slamming my hands on the table. I took a breath and tried to calm myself down, but my heart was pounding. I didn't even know why, to be honest. Of *course* spies were sometimes thieves. They were sometimes assassins and kidnappers and con artists too.

But not my parents. They couldn't be. They were good people . . . even if they weren't here with me and Kennedy . . . because of SRS.

I sighed. Maybe I was lying to myself. Maybe everything in the world really *did* go back to the Sub Rosa Society.

"How about this?" Ben said, very, very tentatively, like he thought I might explode if he spoke too loudly. "I was thinking while I was out today. These books are old, right? Really old. And remember how at Hastings's place, they were in that fancy sort of glass case? Well, that's because they have to be stored in a noble gas."

"A what?" Otter asked impatiently. I could tell he really wanted to get into a yelling match with me. I sort of wanted that too.

"A noble gas," Ben repeated. "They're unreactive, so they're good for things like storing mummies and inflating blimps. Or keeping really old, fancy books in perfect shape."

"So you're saying they might have disintegrated?" Kennedy asked, her eyebrows knitted together like this might break her.

Ben shook his head. "No, I'm saying that whoever has the books has to have a really pure, high-quality noble gas delivered on a regular basis. Not that many individuals do, I bet. So if we just find out who's getting noble gas delivered, we have a whole new list of suspects to look into— people who might have the books *now*, which is really more important than who stole them in the first place, right?"

Everyone mumbled in agreement; Ben and Beatrix exchanged relieved looks. Beatrix placed her fingers over her Right Hand, letting them hover there the way a musician does over a piano. "Noble gas orders?"

"Let's start locally, then branch out. My money's on helium, if you can narrow it—"

"Oh, Bennett," Beatrix said mockingly. "*If* I can narrow it down. *If!*"

Clatterbuck laughed proudly, and Otter, still looking grumpy, leaned over Beatrix's shoulder until she shooed him back to the other side of the table.

"Come on, Kennedy," Walter said to my sister. "Let's practice that stunt. The one where you backflip?"

"Okay," Kennedy said, her face brightening a little, and followed him outside.

I wanted to stay to see what results Beatrix could come up with, but I didn't much want to be in the same room as

Otter at the moment. Kennedy looked surprised to see me step outside behind them—I wasn't usually eager to watch cheerleading, because . . . well, cheerleading. Useful as the occasional lift was, it still wasn't really my style.

"You have to promise not to freak out if you're going to watch us," Kennedy said, looking cautious.

"I swear."

I swore in a different way when Walter basically threw my sister into a backflip, then caught her foot so she was standing on his hands. Kennedy had her hands over her head in a high V, one leg back like a ballerina, and looked pleased.

"Isn't it cool?" she asked. Walter wobbled side to side to keep her balanced above him, his elbows locked out.

"How did you two learn to do that?" I asked.

"There's this video, we saw, and—" She stopped, flipped backward, and landed neatly back in Walter's arms and then did a walkover back to the ground. "It's called a rewind arabesque!"

"Is it . . . uh . . . safe?" I asked.

"So long as I don't miss her on the backflip," Walter said, wiping his hands on his pants.

"We practice it at home over the mats," Kennedy said.

"It looks great. And it looks like Kennedy is a lot easier to throw than I am," I said, smiling and thinking about Walter heaving me over a fence a few weeks prior. Kennedy continued to look pleased, and even though Walter liked to pretend he wasn't into the cheerleading thing, he looked pretty happy too.

Which was a relief, because it meant they hadn't seen my face falter when Kennedy said the word "home." See, when I hear that word, I think about apartment 300 at SRS. I think about the baby-chick-yellow living room, and the secret ice cream compartment in the freezer, and my bedroom with the dinosaur sheets that I always covered when friends came over but actually liked way better than my more grown-up blue-striped sheets.

I didn't think of League headquarters, like Kennedy must. But then, Kennedy had a bedroom full of stuffed animals and cheerleading posters and glitter pens at League headquarters. I had a white bedroom with nothing in it. I wondered where all the stuff I left behind was now. Did SRS stick it in storage? Did they comb through it? Did they burn everything?

I wondered where Mom and Dad were living. Had they made a new home somewhere, like Kennedy, or were they like me? I wasn't sure which one I wanted for them. It was hard to think of them relaxing in some strange living room, eating out of some strange fridge, putting pictures on strange walls. Did they tell jokes and eat ice cream and talk about me and Kennedy, or did they sort of avoid the subject, like Kennedy and I did about them some days? Were they happy even though we weren't with them?

I didn't *think* they could be happy without me and my sister, but then . . . I didn't think they would just leave us behind, either.

I felt bad immediately for thinking that—I mean, what choice did they have? But still . . . I wondered what my life would be like if my parents weren't heroes.

If they were just art thieves.

CHAPTER TWELVE

I went to bed early because I knew I'd never be able to fall asleep after Ben started snoring. That was probably why at about four in the morning I woke up suddenly. I stared at the bunk above me for a while, then tried to count to a million, then tried to clear my mind, but in the end nothing worked. I kicked my legs over the side of the bed, straightened up my pajama pants, and then slipped out of the room to get a glass of water.

To my surprise, the lights were still on in the kitchen. Beatrix was asleep in a chair, exactly where she'd been when I saw her a few hours before. Her computers still buzzed all around her, and her glasses were pushed up on top of her head like a headband.

"Beatrix?" I whispered.

She didn't move.

Whenever Kennedy fell asleep on the couch back home, Dad would carry her to her bed. I was pretty certain I wasn't strong enough to lift Beatrix, but I felt bad that she was going to sleep in a kitchen chair all night. I crept to my bedroom, snatched a blanket off the bunk occupied by Ben's inventing tools, and went back to the kitchen. I tiptoed around Beatrix and tried to slide it over her shoulders . . .

Beatrix sat up and yelped. I clapped a hand over her mouth and tried to spin her so she'd see it was me, but she braced her legs into the table and slammed the chair backward, crushing me between it and the wall. The breath was knocked right out of me, and I'm pretty sure my kidneys had been too—

"Oh! Hale! Oh, I'm sorry!" Beatrix said, yanking the chair off me. "Are you okay?"

I tried to say "I'm fine," but it sounded more like "Iihhii." Beatrix winced with apology, then glanced at the clock.

"Whoa! It's four in the morning. Did I fall asleep?"

"Yes. And apparently you dreamed of ninjas or something," I said, rubbing the spot on my stomach where the chair had dug in.

"Otter said I should learn some basic self-defense," Beatrix said.

"You're excelling at it."

"Really? Yay! I mean—well. Yay, but sorry for smashing your ribs."

"It'll be fine, really." I pointed to her Right Hand. "Any luck with the helium?"

Beatrix's face fell, and she sat back down in her chair. I pulled up one of the others. She said, "Not really, Hale. I mean, plenty of people order helium, but it's the sort of people you'd expect. Blimp companies. The government. Cryogenics companies—did you know that's what they use to cryogenically freeze people? I had no idea. But anyway, there's no one who's ordering a regular supply who isn't someone you'd *expect* to order it, you know?"

I sighed and leaned back in the chair. Then Beatrix said quickly, "I'll keep looking, though!"

"It's okay, Beatrix," I said, shaking my head. "I just don't know where to go from here."

Beatrix bit her lip and tapped her Right Hand absently for a moment. "Maybe we have to look at SRS now, Hale."

"No, that's—"

"Shh! You'll wake everyone up!" she said. I slammed my lips shut—I didn't realize I was shouting. Beatrix and I listened for a moment and, when no one stirred, she beat me to speaking first. "I know it's important to you that your parents have *always* done the right thing, Hale. But you know, it's okay if they messed up. They're still good people, I'm sure."

I waited a long time. Maybe it was because it was dark and the middle of the night, or maybe it was because this was Beatrix, but I closed my eyes and said, "That's not really the problem. Well. Not all of it, anyway."

"What is?"

I opened my eyes and stared at her computer screens, unblinking. If I were being interrogated, my eyes would definitely have given away how uncomfortable all this made me. I reached forward and picked up a screw that had fallen out of one machine or another, rolled it between my forefinger and thumb, and then finally spoke.

"My parents left when they realized SRS was doing something wrong—kidnapping kids for Project Groundcover. But . . . there's no way they couldn't have known stealing art from some little old lady's house was wrong, right? But they did it for years and years, according to Otter. Because that was the mission. You always have to think of the mission at SRS. It's the most important thing."

"Okay . . . ," Beatrix said, nodding, trying to understand.

I went on. "My parents eventually left SRS—which was the right thing to do. But they also left me and Kennedy behind. They didn't warn us or take us with them or come get us after it all blew over. Because they *can't*—their mission, *our* mission, is to take down SRS for good. And if they come get me and Kennedy, the mission could be compromised. So they're thinking of the mission, just like they did at SRS. Putting the mission first. Above everything, even their kids." I drummed my fingers on the table and shook my head. "I get that they're heroes and spies and all, but sometimes I wish they'd just be my parents. I wish we were as important as the stupid mission."

"Hale, I'm sure your parents think you're just as important—*more* important—than the mission! But it's not safe for them to come get you yet," Beatrix said.

I shrugged. "I guess. I mean, I *know* that's true, deep down, but sometimes it doesn't feel very true. And then I get so mad at myself for *getting* mad, because of *course* they should be thinking of the mission!"

"You are always telling the rest of us to put the mission first," Beatrix agreed.

"Right! But then . . . then I'm just acting like I'm back at SRS too. So what's the point of fighting SRS if, in the end, they're too deep inside me for me to ever really escape them? Maybe it's too late for me and my parents and Walter's mom. Maybe we'll always be SRS agents, no matter how hard we fight it."

Beatrix went quiet and put her Right Hand down, which wasn't something she did very often. She turned to face me, even though I still wasn't really looking at her. "Remember how my parents were League agents?"

"Of course."

"And that they died on a mission?"

"Yes. I mean, you and Ben didn't tell us that, but I sort of guessed," I said quietly.

Beatrix folded her legs up underneath her. "I don't really know how it happened or anything—Ben and I were only a year old or so. Uncle Stan says he won't tell us everything till we're older, but I think he really just never wants to think about it. I don't know that I want to know. Ben says he does, but I'm not sure he means it. Anyway— sometimes I'm mad at them. Which is the worst, since they're dead and all, but sometimes I'm mad because they went on that mission. There were a billion other agents at The League back then who could have gone, agents without kids. Why did *they* have to do it?"

I didn't say anything. I didn't know what *to* say. I understood what she meant, and I thought I understood how she felt, but there was just no fixing it.

Beatrix took a long breath. "If they'd known what would happen, I'm sure they wouldn't have gone. And if your parents had known how long they'd have to be away from you and Kennedy, I bet they wouldn't have gone either. Just because they're parents doesn't mean they can't make mistakes. And just because they're SRS agents doesn't mean they love the mission more than you. They were all just trying to be heroes."

I nodded because she was right, and then I sighed. "I always wanted to be a hero, you know. Like them. But I don't think I want to be the kind of hero who leaves my family behind. Does that make me a terrible person?"

Beatrix smiled. "No. It just makes you a regular person, I think."

I nodded. Then after a long time I said, "I'm sorry about your parents, Beatrix."

"Yeah, I know," she said, and smiled. "But it's okay. We're all okay. Also, we're all tired. Seriously, Hale, your eyes look like someone punched you. Unless—were you trying to help Kennedy with that cheerleading pyramid she wants to do? Because Ben tried a few weeks ago, and she kicked him right in the eye on accident."

"No—just tired," I said, and smiled too. I stood up and pushed my chair in. "Are you going to bed?"

"I guess so. I'll run everything through the system again tomorrow just to make sure I didn't miss anything. But . . . do you think maybe we can look into SRS now that the noble gases turned up nothing?" she asked.

I bit my tongue for a second, because I was thinking, *Of course we can—mission first, right?* Then I let my fingertips linger on the list of partygoers that rested on the edge of the table. "Yes. Of course, yes . . . but can I go over these people one more time to make *sure* they're dead ends?"

Beatrix sighed a little—her talk, however moving, however sincere, hadn't gotten to me quite as completely as she hoped it would. "You can do whatever you want, Hale. But you trust me, right? I went over them all."

"Of course I trust you; I just . . . I just want to be sure, I guess. It's not even because I don't want to look into SRS. It's that I feel like I missed something." Once I said it aloud, the feeling grew stronger—that gut feeling that SRS had taught us to trust.

Beatrix lifted her Right Hand. "Well, let's go over it together. So, we ruled out all the employees, right? Ben and Kennedy felt pretty confident about those."

"Okay, yeah."

"And then . . . we have the three families from Hastings's birthday party who live in other countries, but I picked through their bank accounts. No sign of an influx of money, and no sign of sudden helium buying."

"All right, yes . . ."

"And then there are the country club families. I checked them for helium buying too, but you also cleared the Stonemans, the Alabasters, and . . . what was that final name?"

"The St. Claires."

"Oh, right, the ones who made fun of Hastings for having a clown at his birthday party—"

Beatrix nearly dropped her Right Hand. Our eyes snapped together and widened in sync. The paper slipped from my fingers.

"Access to helium. Attended the birthday party. *The clown*," I said under my breath. "We never looked into the clown."

CHAPTER THIRTEEN

Because it was a weekday, we couldn't talk to Hastings about the clown until that evening, when he'd arrived home from the bank. There wasn't much to do on the *poney* farm other than look at the aforementioned ponies, so we—everyone but Beatrix and Ben, who stayed behind to source uranium for something or another—got to Hastings's early, broke in, and made sandwiches. Clatterbuck worried Hastings might be mad at us, using up his groceries. Otter wasn't worried; he said Hastings owed us a break-in and a few sandwiches, given that we'd been in Switzerland for a week now just for him.

"Cheese is Annabelle's favorite," Kennedy said fondly, feeding the dog another cheese sandwich. I think this was number four. Maybe five? It was hard to count, since Annabelle had smashed her entire body onto my lap and her giant head blocked most of my view. Annabelle swallowed her sandwich, then looked back at me with wistful eyes; I patted her head again, because even though she was sort of suffocating me, it was sort of impossible to say no to those eyes.

"What's the next trick you're teaching her?" I asked.

"Fetch, maybe? She'll run after the ball, but she won't bring it back. Watch—"

Kennedy grabbed a tennis ball from the ground, and before I could stop her, she reeled her arm back. Annabelle leaped off me in a flurry of oh-my-gosh-time-to-play! enthusiasm, kicking me squarely in the stomach as she did so.

"Oh! Sorry, Hale—ah!" Kennedy crumbled to the ground as Annabelle grabbed for the ball in her hand. They wrestled for it, and Annabelle won, pinning Kennedy to the floor and licking her face happily.

"I liked her better when she was a floor cushion," Otter said. I would have argued that Annabelle would probably like him better as a floor cushion, but I was pretty sure the dog had rearranged my internal organs with that jump, and I was having trouble finding my lungs.

The front door opened; everyone stood except for Kennedy, who rolled Annabelle off her and was just scrambling to her feet when Hastings walked in.

"Finally! Tell us everything you know about the clown!" I said.

Hastings leaped into the air, flinging his briefcase to the ceiling. It cracked when it hit the ground, and papers flew up, then drifted down slowly like office-themed confetti.

"How'd you get in here?" he asked, clutching his heart. I guess arriving home to seven people in your kitchen can be a little disarming, especially when you're working for a major crime organization.

"Spies? Remember?" I said. "Anyway, there was a clown at your birthday party. We cleared everyone else who was there, and your old staff, but the clown—"

"What are you eating?" he asked, frowning.

"We made you one," Kennedy said without answering the question, and shoved a cheese sandwich I was certain she'd made for Annabelle his way.

Hastings gave her a strange look, then took it as he collapsed into an expensive-looking leather recliner. "Okay, clown. A clown. *The* clown. I . . . I don't remember. I was twelve!"

"I remember *my* twelfth birthday," Walter said, looking bitter. He'd spent most of the afternoon watching French television. But since his French wasn't so great, he'd been unable to understand more than a few passing words.

Hastings scowled at him. "That's because you're what, thirteen, at the most? I remember he was a *clown!*"

"Perhaps in your grandmother's financial records, we can find where she paid him?" Otter said, his voice tense.

Hastings shrugged. "I don't know. I don't really understand financial stuff."

"You're a *banker*," Walter and I said at the same time.

"I know how to move money around accounts! But my grandmother always handled *our* finances!" Hastings said, throwing his hands into the air.

"It's amazing you still have a dime," Otter said drily. "Fine—do you remember *anything* else? What sort of car did he drive? Was he from a company, or more of a self-employed individual clown?"

"I think he was just an individual. I remember his makeup? Sort of . . . red here . . . white there . . . purple . . . ," Hastings said, waving his hands a bit. "I'd know the makeup if I saw it again, I'm sure." Annabelle, who'd been watching his sandwich carefully, dived forward and glommed her mouth onto it. Hastings recoiled, looking disgusted. "Hey! Bad dog! Cheese is bad for your fur!"

Kennedy's eyes widened. She edged the nearly gone block of cheese behind some canisters.

I lifted my comm mic to my mouth. "Beatrix, are you there? Can you tell me how many photos of Swiss clowns there are on the Internet? We've got to somehow find a photo of this clown."

"Huh? Oh, yeah, I'm here—hang on, Hale, I'm trying to steady this tray of aluminum pegs. Okay . . . okay . . . all right, here we go—Swiss clowns?" Beatrix asked. I heard Ben muttering in the background, which usually meant the invention was coming along nicely. "There are about a billion photos when I search for 'Swiss clown.'"

"What about 'Swiss clown makeup'?"

"There are . . . huh. A little less than a billion. Sorry, Hale, it's just that lots of random stuff gets tagged with the word "clown." Why?"

"Isn't there some sort of clown database or registry or something that you can hack?" Otter asked, pacing back and forth in front of Hastings.

"Searching . . . ," Beatrix said. "Yes! There . . . oh."

"'Oh' what?" I asked.

"Well, there *is* a clown database. But it's physical. I can't hack it," Beatrix answered. "It's in Somerset."

"England?" I asked.

"Will one of you tell me what she's saying?" Hastings said, pouting. Without a comm, he couldn't hear Beatrix.

I sighed—Hastings had never been a very sympathetic guy, but the whining was pushing me over the edge.

"Beatrix, I'll get back to you," I said; then to Hastings, "There's a registry of clown face paintings, but it's in England."

"So you're going to England?" Hastings said, sounding pleased.

"No," Otter said firmly. He took a few steps toward Hastings, and for a moment I thought Otter might slap the guy. Instead Otter put his hands on his hips and lifted his chin—a technique that made him look taller than he actually was, one that we learned back at SRS. "Mr. Hastings, I'm growing a little tired of being your personal loss recovery department, all on the promise that if we find these books, you'll give us information so we can *hopefully* rob SRS's bank account."

"You offered!" Hastings protested, throwing his hands around again. Annabelle looked up, but seeing there was no longer a sandwich to gobble, she snorted and leaned so hard against Kennedy, they both toppled over.

Otter shook his head. "We offered to find the books, sure—when we thought it was a simple research job. But we're not going to England without some sort of guarantee that when this is done, you'll come through on your end."

"Well, maybe then, maybe I'll just say never mind and you can go home and I'll just stick with Annabelle," Hastings said haughtily.

Now, look: I'm not proud of this. But I *already* didn't like Hastings much, what with how he sold all his grandmother's stuff, and how he basically just wanted the books back so he could have even *more* money when he was already making a half million dollars per puppy off Annabelle. All that combined meant Hastings's threat didn't really sit too well with me.

So, while Kennedy, Walter, and Otter were looking shocked and offended, I said, coolly, "You're forgetting,

Mr. Hastings, that we *also* can tell the world about Annabelle's heritage."

Hastings blanched. "What? No! You wouldn't. You're supposed to be the good guys! That's what you told me!"

"And we are. Which is why we have to get those account numbers, Mr. Hastings. We're willing to help you in order to get them, but we are not willing to let you walk away entirely," Otter said.

"Well . . . I . . ." Hastings fumbled between words and emotions—first he looked angry, then upset, then panicked. Finally he shouted, "*Fine. Just fine.* What do you want, then?"

"Annabelle. As collateral," I said, folding my arms.

"The *dog*?" Hastings said. "She's worth millions!"

"Then she's excellent collateral," Otter said. "We'll take good care of her, right, everyone?" He turned to Kennedy and Walter as he said this. They looked a little uncomfortable with the whole exchange, but they nodded.

"She likes us, Mr. Hastings. We'll take good care of her," Kennedy said earnestly.

"She doesn't like anyone—she hardly even does anything," Hastings argued grumpily. "Fine. Take the dumb dog. But you'll go to England, then?"

Otter sighed and put his fingers to his forehead, which was something he did more and more these days. "We'll send a team to England to look at the clown registry, and we will be in touch with you."

The fact that Hastings didn't seem sad at all about Annabelle coming to the farmhouse helped the niggling guilt I felt burrowing around in my gut over the fact that we'd basically just kidnapped the guy's pet. I'd hoped his reaction would sway Kennedy and Walter as well, but they looked a little testy on the bus home.

Annabelle, on the other hand, looked like she'd just won some sort of dog lottery. Her eyes were big, her mouth was open and panting, and she kept laying her head in our laps, going from person to person like she was inspecting us each for general petting abilities.

On Annabelle's second pass, I rubbed her ears together and looked up at my sister. "Okay, Kennedy. I get it. But I don't think Annabelle is sad to leave Hastings. I mean, *look* at her. He didn't even like her, and I don't think she liked him, either."

"That's not it, Hale," Kennedy said hesitantly, like she didn't want to argue but couldn't keep the words in for long. "It's just . . . well. Taking the dog as collateral is just . . . it's something SRS would do. We're not supposed to be like them."

Otter jumped in. "That man would have had us go to England—go all over Europe, really—to find his books. We're not messengers, and we're not personal assistants. We're spies. Sometimes deals have to be made," Otter said, keeping his voice low—we were on a public bus, after all, and the Swiss people all around us already looked kind of perplexed by the giant dog in their midst.

Walter and Kennedy went quiet. I stayed quiet. Because I hadn't even thought about that—that taking the dog was something SRS would do. I'd thought of the mission. I'd thought of how we had to do something to keep from being Hastings's voluntary treasure hunters. I'd thought of how we had to move faster, to rob the bank. I'd thought exactly like SRS had trained me to think, but . . . it was what had to be done, wasn't it? Were we allowed to act like the bad guys in order to be the good guys in the end?

When we got home, Kennedy fed Annabelle all the sausages Clatterbuck had been planning to make us for dinner. Otter shouted at her, then I shouted at Otter, and then Annabelle started to howl, and then Ben's newest invention—the TurBENate—exploded in the yard, and we had to spend most of the evening convincing the couple who owned the pony farm that it was just a meteor, not dynamite strapped to a station-wagon bumper. When they left, we all reconvened for a moment in the kitchen to eat crackers and the buns that were supposed to go with the sausages.

Otter said, "Beatrix, I need everything you've got on that clown database. How to break in, how to—"

"Oh, you won't have to break in. They're all on display!"

Otter blinked.

"At . . . a place in Somerset called Wookey Hole Caves?"

We all blinked.

"That's what it's called! They're on display there. You can buy tickets. We could all go! There's a dinosaur exhibit!" Beatrix said, growing more excited. Ben was nodding enthusiastically.

"It's not a game!" Otter snapped. What was strange about this is that he didn't yell. He just said it, *bam*, like a quick punch, and it threw everyone. He put his fingers to his temples. "I'm going to bed. Jordan and I are going to Somerset tomorrow. Clatterbuck, set up a transport, please. Ben, we'll need hidden cameras, and Beatrix, we'll need a live feed at Hastings's. Got it?"

Everyone nodded without saying anything.

CHAPTER FOURTEEN

Our team was *always* pretty quick (we had to be, since it was just the seven of us), but the trip to Wookey Hole Caves came together in record time. Before bed, Beatrix and Ben had put together a new round of fake passports. By the next morning, Clatterbuck had arranged for a flight to Bristol, and a rental car for when we arrived—something sporty, which I think he got to try to improve Otter's mood. Annabelle had greeted each and every one of us that morning—including Otter—by leaping onto us and licking our faces.

Otter's just not the sort of guy whose face you lick, but I guess Annabelle didn't know that yet.

"These are pretty basic," Ben said as we ate cereal for breakfast. He opened a pair of glasses and reached across the table to slide them onto my face. "They plug right into your comm, so they'll use the same system. The camera is in the center, which is why I had to put the tape there. Sorry, Hale."

There was, indeed, a thick strip of tape in the center of the glasses, which were already huge and old-person-like. I looked over at Beatrix's Right Hand—there was a little black-and-white video of everything I saw playing in the center.

"Looks good?" she asked.

"Looks great. You'll take this over to Hastings's place once we get there?"

"Yep! And if we have extra time, I'm going to try to squeeze in one of those helicopter tours today. You think there'll be time?" Clatterbuck said, rolling a ball back and forth between his hands for Annabelle, who was just a little too slow to actually catch it but very entertained by trying.

"I doubt it. But I'll hurry, okay?" I promised, patting Clatterbuck on the back when he went crestfallen.

Otter didn't really talk to me on the way to the Geneva airport. Once we were there, he went totally into character, pretending to be my father. I figured when we were on the plane, he'd at least want to go over the mission, simple as it was, but he read a German magazine from the seat-back pocket instead. I used the time to memorize flight patterns, since that seemed like the sort of information a spy might use one day.

We landed in Bristol, which was rainy and cool. Otter's car was red and small and looked sort of desperate, if you ask me, but it *did* seem to improve his mood. He almost smiled when we cut through bright-green countryside. The road was tiny, nestled between hills and trees and stone walls, and Otter took corners fast so that it pinned us both to our seats. We passed quaint lodges and inns, and the occasional dog ran out of a cottage and chased our car for a ways. Finally we arrived at a cluster of neat buildings made of stone and stucco, one of which had a roof that looked like a witch's hat. Also, there was a giant gorilla statue.

"This is the place?" Otter asked warily, looking at the gorilla's head. Behind it, there was a handful of stone dinosaur heads. "I thought they were like, *caves*. You know. Underground."

"The website said they have lots of stuff. Caves and an arcade and a Christmas show . . . ," I began.

"And a clown registry?" Otter said.

"I guess. Beatrix? You with me?" I said over the comm as I put my glasses on.

"We're here! Well. Me and Ben and Uncle Stan. Kennedy and Walter are trying to take Annabelle for a walk, but she won't leave the front step," Beatrix said in my ear.

"All right. Let's go," I said. I paused for a moment to look at the way the other kids my age were approaching the front gate, then: "Come on! We're going to miss the circus!" I whined loudly.

"I'm *coming*," Otter grumbled in a parental sort of way. He pressed the button to lock the car and then trudged behind me as I bounded to the gate. I wished I'd thought to get some ice cream stains on my shirt to complete the character; instead I ruffled my hair so that it stood on end, like I'd been sleeping on a long car ride. We weren't really pulling one over on anyone for this mission, but I couldn't help but get the details down.

"One adult and one child?" a lady in a witch costume asked at the front counter. Otter flashed a fake season pass card—Clatterbuck made it himself last night—and in we went.

"I'd really like to see the clown registry. Don't think we've made it down there before. Can you point me in the right direction?" Otter asked pleasantly in a flawless London accent. Meanwhile, I grabbed ahold of his arm and made a show of pulling him farther into the park. It wasn't my most dignified character, but spy work wasn't always dignified.

"The clown registry?" the witch asked, frowning. "You mean—oh! The eggs! Not many people come just to see those. Down this way, then a right, in the circus area. They'll be right in front of you."

"Thanks," Otter said to the witch, and then over his comm, "Eggs? What's that about, Beatrix?"

"It's Ben—Annabelle got out and is chasing the ponies, so Beatrix and Kennedy are trying to catch her and they slipped in a pile of— Never mind. So, apparently the clown database is stored on eggs."

"I have no idea what you mean," I said into my comm.

"They're *on* eggs. It's how they kept—"

"Ohhhhh," Otter and I said at once, because as soon as we ducked into the Wookey Hole circus tent, we saw just what Ben meant.

There were hundreds of eggs set up in little rows in a case lined with red velvet. Each egg was immaculately painted with a clown's face. The level of detail was amazing—gruff and speckled beards, bright eyes, hats, and even tufts of hair were glued onto the eggshells. The pedestals the eggs rested on were made to look like the tops of the clowns' shirts, and in front of those were little placards with each clown's name on them.

It was one of the coolest things I'd ever seen, and also one of the creepiest. All those little clown eyes staring at me, frozen smiles and garish makeup. It didn't help that there were three life-size clown mannequins nearby.

"*Hi there!*" one of the mannequins shouted.

Otter screamed. He told everyone afterward that it wasn't a scream, it was just the comm mic reverberating, but I was there and I promise, he screamed.

The mannequin—who was not a mannequin after all— jumped off the platform. The other two mannequins who apparently *were* mannequins stayed put.

"Come to see the show?" the clown asked in a bobbly voice, squeezing a flower-shaped horn affixed to his giant coat.

"We came to see these, actually," I said, motioning to the eggs.

The clown's face softened, even under all the makeup. "The egg registry? No one ever comes to see the egg registry!"

"It's for a school project," I said swiftly, even though it made me sad when the clown's face fell a little. Still, he seemed touched.

"Well! Do you need any help?" the clown asked, pulling at his suspenders and rocking back on his heels.

"Oh no, we're—"

"Hale! They don't show the clowns' real names on the displays—they keep those in a book in the back. So maybe play nice with the clown," Beatrix said, her voice rushed like she'd run back to the comm. Or, more likely, rushed like she'd just shoved a one-hundred-and-fifty-pound dog off Walter.

"You know, I did have a few questions, actually," I said swiftly, and smiled as goofily as I could. People liked goofy. It put them at ease. Probably why clowns were so popular—though, given Otter's still blanched face, I guessed they didn't put *everyone* at ease.

I asked a few questions just to get the clown talking; he took us back and forth, pointing to famous clowns here and there. I let my eyes drift over each egg, going slowly so the camera in my glasses could focus properly. At each one, I heard Hastings in the background back in Geneva. "No. No. Maybe! No, wait, no . . ."

"A whole bunch were broken when a display cabinet fell and crushed them. Goose eggs are tough, but they're not *that* tough," the clown showing us around said sadly, shaking his head. I stepped to the next case.

"That's him!" Hastings roared so loud, the comm earpiece squealed.

I flinched. The clown heard Hastings; there was no doubt. And he was frowning, which was weird since his face was still painted into a smile. He looked up at the ceiling, toward the speakers that played circusy music quietly.

"I love this clown's makeup. Do you know who he is?" I asked casually, pointing to Twinkles Meatloaf.

"Uh . . . I . . ." The clown was still looking around, confused, but then he refocused. "Twinkles Meatloaf. Now *that's* a name," he said, though I couldn't tell if this was a compliment or not. "Anyway—now, see, no other clown is allowed to use his face makeup *or* his name because he's registered himself here!"

"Cool! So what would he do if he caught another clown using his face makeup?" I asked overenthusiastically.

"Well, he'd most likely try to settle it with the other clown first—sometimes mistakes happen. But if they couldn't work it out, he could call a lawyer, who would come here and check the book in the back to verify that

Twinkles Meatloaf was registered. So, let's say you become a clown—"

Annabelle started barking over my headset—loudly. The clown froze again, and I saw his eyes on my head, tracking the sound's source—

"*Whoa whoa whoa!*" Otter cried. "What are you trying to do, mister? Talking to my son about becoming a *clown*?"

"Huh?" the clown said, blinking. I heard a clattering as everyone back in Geneva tried to silence the dog, but it only made things louder.

"Well, first it's jumping out at us from the mannequin display, then it's all the information on the eggs, then it's all the details on the clown registry—he's going to be a lawyer, right, son?" Otter boomed, talking fast to cover up Annabelle's barks.

"Uh, sorry, sir. I was just trying to help him with his report—"

"I know how you clowns operate! First it's a joke here, a water-squirting flower there, and the next thing you know, *indoctrination!*"

The clown was floored. He looked at me, then at Otter, then back at me, then said, "Perhaps I should go get my manager—"

"I'll bet he's a clown too!"

"No, no. He's the ringmaster. I'll be right back. Let me get him . . . ," the clown said, backing out of the room slowly. He'd barely made it out the door when Otter turned to me.

"I'm going!" I said, and slunk around the egg display and into a room labeled EMPLOYEES ONLY.

It was tiny—barely more than an office—and covered in vintage circus posters. I squinted in the dim light—then nearly screamed like Otter, because suddenly there was someone right in front of me. *No, no, calm down*—it was just a mannequin dressed in a clown suit but without any makeup on. His weirdly blank face watched me as I yanked out one of Ben's inventions—the BEN of All Trades, which was basically a Swiss Army knife with all the stuff Ben deemed necessary attached. There was the typical stuff, like little scissors and a flashlight, but he'd also included a rubber band shooter and a whisk, which I'd never had the opportunity to use. I flicked on the flashlight, held the BEN of All Trades by the whisk, and peered at the thick books that lined one wall.

Most were old yearbooks from a local clown college, or crumbling guides on applying face paint. A few folders looked like old tax records, and there were some phone books from before I was born stacked high in one corner. The books were clearly seldom used—while they were lined up neatly enough, the space between them and the shelf above was crammed with receipts, face paint containers, makeup sponges, and stacks of unsorted paperwork. I leaned in closer. I could hear Otter grumbling outside, then his voice raise as the clown—and ringmaster—reappeared.

There! A binder, the sort regular kids used in school, with a scratchily written label on the side: *Clown Database Copy.* I slipped it out of its spot and begin to flip through it frantically. Twinkles Meatloaf, Twinkles Meatloaf . . . The registry seemed to be sorted by the clowns' real names rather than their stage ones, which meant I had to do this one page at a time . . .

"My point is, there should be some sort of advisory on the front of this tent! 'Parents: clowns within will try to convert your child!'" Otter bellowed.

"Sir, I'm sure Noodle here was just—"

"*Noodle?* What manner of good Christian name is *Noodle?*"

"It's a clown name, sir—"

I took a deep breath and blocked them out. I ran my finger down the list of clowns' names—Ernie Burch, George Carl, Barry Lubin, a million people with the last name Fratellini. I still hadn't seen a real name for Twinkles Meatloaf, and I suspected the ringmaster was about to call security on Otter.

"There!" I whispered frantically into my comm. "I've got it. Twinkles Meatloaf. Real name Kevin Stroganoff. Last known address Chemin Jacques-Attenville, 13C, 1352 Le Grand-Sacconex."

"That's in Geneva!" Hastings said excitedly. Ben, Beatrix, and Clatterbuck shushed him.

"Got it, Hale. Anything else?" Beatrix asked.

"There's no phone number, says he's been a member of the registry since—"

"And now he's lost in your clown-land building!" Otter shouted, his voice rising in a way that was undoubtedly meant to signal me. I slammed the book shut and closed the BEN of All Trades. Footsteps were coming, growing closer and closer to the door—I snatched a wig and jammed it onto my head, then grabbed a handful of face makeup.

"*Mon dieu!*" the ringmaster and the clown said at the same time.

Otter said something less eloquent and then jumped back into his tirade. "See? Look what you've done to him!"

The wig was on crooked, but I'd managed to slather a fair amount of white paint onto my face. I had a blue diamond around each eye—well, they were diamondish, anyhow. My attempt at putting red around my lips had been foiled by the door swinging open, so rather than a cherry-red mouth, it just looked like someone had socked me in the teeth. I caught a glimpse of myself in one of the glass cases behind the three adults. I'm not sure "atrocious" really covers how I looked.

"All I did was tell him about the eggs!" the clown said, throwing his red-gloved hands into the air. The white paint around his eyes made him look even more shocked than he was. The ringmaster, dressed in a red coat with tails, looked like he wished he'd called in sick today. The man's mustache quivered as Otter grabbed the back of my shirt.

"We're *leaving*, Hector!" Otter said.

"But I want to *be a clown*!" I wailed as he dragged me along, nearly dislodging my earpiece with his enthusiasm. The clown snatched the wig off my head as I passed them; I glanced back to see him and the ringmaster watching us go with some combination of fear and pity. Otter hauled me back down the path, past confused visitors; I tried to wipe my face off as we went but only succeeded in smudging all the makeup around. When we finally got into the car, it looked like I'd rubbed my face in pastel purple icing.

"Hale? Agent Otter? Are you still there?" Beatrix asked.

"*Director* Otter," Otter corrected.

I ignored him. "We're here. We're out. On our way back now."

Beatrix said, "Perfect. By the time you get back, I should have Twinkles Meatloaf's financials and history pulled up and ready."

"Is he still a . . . uh . . . practicing clown?" I asked.

"Looks that way. Though, whoa. Dude is old and cragily looking."

I pulled up the edge of my shirt and made another attempt to wipe some of the face paint off (it didn't work) and then said, "Perfect. Because we'll need to book a performance."

CHAPTER FIFTEEN

On the flight home, we were upgraded to first class because the lady at the gate desk thought my still slightly blue face was a symptom of some serious medical condition and felt sorry for me. I wasn't about to argue, since first class meant better snacks and less arm-to-arm contact with Otter. He sat down and immediately ordered two glasses of wine that smelled like cheap pink candy. I got a Coke and ate some cookies, watching England vanish into the English Channel.

"Your English accent needs work," Otter said. I rolled my eyes and didn't say anything, because frankly, my English accent was better than his. He was just good at making his sound more London than I was. Otter went on, "We should hit up Twinkles's house tomorrow. Then we're ready for the bank." One day was a quick turnaround, but seeing how quickly the trip to Wookey Hole came together, a simple break-in couldn't be out of our reach.

As we crossed over into France, Otter removed a yellow legal pad from his bag and began to write up a mission report on Wookey Hole. No one would be reading it other than him, of course, but he still did them for every mission, even the practice ones we did back at League headquarters. I wasn't sure if he ever went over them, or if he just did it because it was what he would've done at SRS. I sort of understood, to be honest. Writing up a mission report was like putting the period on the end of the sentence. Get all the details down and boom, you're done—you can forget about it and focus on finding some dinner. I hadn't done it since starting at The League, but I sort of wanted to. I always stopped myself, though—in part because Otter would want to collect and read them, just like any agency director would, and in part because it felt too much like SRS creeping back into my life, dictating my likes and dislikes and habits and schedule.

"Don't you worry about doing that?" I asked.

Otter looked up at me and then frowned. "Huh?"

I did my best to keep my face even, to hide any trace of emotion—like I was just asking the answer to a math problem. "Don't you worry about doing things the way SRS did them? Like writing up mission reports. You don't have to do that, but SRS trained you to do it."

"So do I worry I'm still an SRS puppet?" Otter asked, and there wasn't any trace of sneer in his voice, which surprised me a little. I nodded, and Otter flipped his notebook over and exhaled. "Here's the thing, Jordan, the thing that no one wants to say—SRS is good at their jobs. They're the best spies in the world. They create the best spies in the world. You think most nine-year-old girls understand the finer points of explosives engineering? No, but Kennedy does. There's a reason SRS was able to ruin The League all those years ago, and it's because they're *better* than The League. So to beat SRS, we'll have to use what we learned there. They're the best."

"Okay, sure, using what we learned. But you're writing mission reports. You don't have to write mission reports for anyone, but SRS is in your brain, they've made it so you *have* to do that when you finish a mission," I said.

Otter stopped and then looked at his notebook. He raised his eyebrows a little and then shrugged. "I do mission reports for myself. But maybe you're right. Maybe I don't know the difference between myself and the SRS agent."

That wasn't the answer I wanted to hear, and it tugged at my nerves that Otter sounded so cavalier about the whole thing. I turned away so he couldn't tell all that from my face, but I suspected he figured it out anyhow.

A flight attendant in a sharp red uniform came by, refilling drinks. When she had passed, Otter dropped his voice and said, "Let's arrange a performance from that clown tomorrow so we can scope out his house and get the books. If we're right, if they're there . . ." He shook his head. "Maybe this was a mistake. Maybe we shouldn't have tried a bank heist so early on. I figured it was actually easier, since it didn't involve uncovering SRS's current missions—it just involved figuring out a bank's weak points. But it's impossible to plan anything here. I think, oh—we'll get three agents on the job, give them a few tanks and an armored car—but wait, no. We don't have tanks, and we have to rent cars. Or I think, okay, we'll set up a giant fake server—but wait, we don't have the server power to duplicate the Russian Internet. Or I think, hey, it's fine, I'll sleep on it and ask for someone else to weigh in. But wait, there is no one else." He downed the rest of his wine and then put the plastic cup on his tray table and stared at it.

"Eventually some other agents will come over, I'm sure," I said. "That'll help."

"What, like Walter's mom?" Otter asked warily. In a weird way it was a relief to see he thought Mrs. Quaddlebaum joining us was just as unlikely as I did. Otter went on, "You know, I actually thought once we got out, your parents would swoop in? They'd take you and Kennedy and Walter, and then I'd go into hiding somewhere, and Clatterbuck and the twins could go be normal in . . . I dunno. Pittsburgh or something. No, someplace where people wear lots of weird costumes. New York. Clatterbuck'd be at home in New York."

I turned away from him and looked straight ahead to answer. "Well. I thought that too. About my parents, I mean."

Otter shook his head and sighed. "They'll come back eventually though."

"When is *eventually*?" I asked.

Otter raised an eyebrow at me, like he wasn't sure we should be having this sort of conversation. "When they can, Jordan."

I scoffed. "Well. Let's hope they can get around to it sometime soon." I immediately felt a little bad for saying that out loud, but Otter wasn't like Kennedy or Walter—I didn't have to pretend to be all hopeful for him. We sat in silence for a few minutes.

"Well. I'll say this, at least—I never thought I'd hope for the day Katie and Joseph Jordan would walk through my door," Otter finally muttered, sounding disgusted with himself.

"Never hoped for the day I'd be on an overseas mission with you as my partner," I answered, and Otter pretended to clink his empty plastic cup against my empty Coke can in cheers.

Clatterbuck was waiting for us at the airport, dressed as a chauffeur and holding a sign that said INTERNATIONAL

SWISS CLOWN COMMITTEE. I wasn't entirely sure why he couldn't just meet us in the parking lot with the car, but that was really just Clatterbuck's style. Plus, I think he liked wearing the chauffeur's hat. We arrived back at the farmhouse just as Ben and Kennedy finished half burning a frozen pizza in the oven.

"It's not my fault! I got distracted because, *Hale*, I taught Annabelle a really great trick!" she said, beaming—then coughing a little from inhaling the burnt pizza smoke.

"Did you teach her to order delivery pizza?" Otter asked flatly.

Kennedy's enthusiasm couldn't be dampened. "No, watch!" She picked off a particularly crispy piece of pizza crust. Annabelle, having already jumped at me and Otter gleefully, was now standing by with pleading eyes and smacking lips. "Annabelle, lie down," Kennedy said calmly. Annabelle obeyed, though her eyes got somehow even more pleading.

I smiled supportively and nodded. "You taught her to lie dow—"

"We're not done," Kennedy said. "Annabelle, play dead!"

Annabelle rolled onto her back and stuck all four feet in the air. It was an impressive enough rendition of "dead" that even Otter made an approving noise.

"How'd you teach her that?" I asked.

"It was easy! She's not really in great shape, so after we brought her back in from chasing the ponies, this is what she did for about an hour. I just started giving her treats and then adding commands."

Otter sighed and pulled the least-charred slice of pizza away from the other pieces. The rest of us fixed our plates (and opened a few windows for the smoke) while Otter and I explained our next steps.

"You're breaking into Twinkles's house tomorrow?" Beatrix asked when we were finished. "Isn't that a little fast? If you give me a few days, I bet Ben and I can piece together house blueprints based on satellite photos. Or we can probably find the actual blueprints, if they're still on file with the city."

"It's a simple smash-and-grab job, I'm sure," I said, shaking my head at her. "Don't worry about it. We'll call and say we have an emergency birthday party or something. Twinkles comes here, we'll go in there, find the helium chamber, grab the books, and go."

"It's best if you move them into another helium chamber. Maybe I can rig up something in the trunk? But overnight . . . huh. Well. I can just skip sleep," Ben said thoughtfully.

"I'll arrange a rental car for you to drive there in, since having priceless books on the city bus is probably a bad idea," Clatterbuck said.

"What about cameras? Or alarms?" Kennedy asked.

"Cameras won't matter—he can't call the police, because he stole the books to start with—but sure, we should be prepared for them just in case. And alarms . . . Well, if he's *here*, it'll take him at least an hour to get back and check the alarms if they signal him," I said.

"But what if they're just regular house alarms you set off, the sort that call the police, because he doesn't have the books?" Clatterbuck asked.

"He has them," I said.

"Well, most likely, but I still think it's a little strange that a clown would steal priceless books *and* store them for years," Clatterbuck said.

"He has them," I repeated, and turned to face him. "All signs point to this guy, okay? It makes a lot more sense for a third party to have them than SRS, anyway."

"Okay," Clatterbuck said, nodding. I could tell he wasn't entirely convinced. That he still thought SRS might have the books, that my parents might have been the ones to steal them so many years ago.

But no. SRS already had my parents and my past and my foreseeable future. SRS even had my *stuff*—my house, my bedspread, the rocks Dad brought me back from that mission to a Peruvian volcano.

They couldn't have the books too.

CHAPTER SIXTEEN

Mission: Steal back the Runanko
Books from Twinkles Meatloaf

"We're letting *this* guy in the farmhouse?" Kennedy said, staring at the website. Twinkles Meatloaf—er, Kevin Stroganoff—looked like his skin was melting off his face. His makeup was patchy, and even his wig seemed to have thinning hair. There were no photos of him without his clown getup, but if the made-up versions were any indication, he wasn't exactly a looker. I wasn't especially afraid of clowns, but this guy could very well change all that.

"We won't need much time," I said, pulling a shirt over my old SRS uniform. This was just a simple break-in, but still, I felt like it was wise to have the uniform on under my clothes—or maybe it just made me feel more like a real spy. Kennedy and Walter were wearing theirs as well; Kennedy's had become a bit snug, given her growth spurt over the summer. She closed the laptop she'd been looking at and handed it to Beatrix. We were clearing all of Beatrix's computer stuff out of the kitchen so Twinkles wouldn't see it when he arrived.

The back door opened, and Ben, Clatterbuck, and Otter walked in, Annabelle trailing them with what looked like a dismembered robot arm in her mouth.

Ben grinned. "It's from one of my older model robots, don't worry. Anyway, helium tanks are installed in the back of the car, Hale. Should be all set to safely hold the books until we can get them back to Hastings." He motioned for me, Walter, and Kennedy to gather around him. "All right, so, chances are that the books are in a helium chamber, just like they were at Hastings's. If you can get into the tank legitimately—pick the lock or something—it'll probably turn the helium pump off. But if you have to just shatter it or bust it up, the mechanism won't flip the helium off, and it'll fill the whole room with helium. Depending on the size of the room, that can be really dicey—the helium will rise to the top of the room, just like a helium-filled balloon floats up. Assuming the room has an average height ceiling for the homes in the area, that means, you"—he pointed to Walter—"will be too tall to stay in the oxygen. You'll be breathing pure helium."

"And that's bad," Walter said.

"Very. You'll suffocate. So I made you this out of scuba gear and some vacuum tubes," Ben said. He reached to the side of the couch and grabbed a little canister with a long hose attached to something that looked like a hacked-up scuba mask. "Put this over your mouth. The pump takes the air—the oxygen, really—from around your feet and sends it up the tube to your head. It's called the B(reathe)-EN."

"Whoa," Walter said. "Thanks."

"I went ahead and put together your belts with the stuff I think you're most likely to need—the basics, of course, and then a few odds and ends. You've got the CariBENer, the DustBEN, the BEN of All Trades. There's also a can of spray paint, just in case he has cameras you need to take out."

That wasn't really how I would take out a camera— I'd likely just unhook it rather than blacken the screen— but a lot of Ben's spy knowledge still came from movies. I nodded and took my utility belt from him. Kennedy had fewer items on hers—since she was usually the one who had to slink in places, she couldn't carry around a lot of tools. Walter's belt was nearly entirely taken up by the B(reathe)-EN, which made him look a little like he'd decided to go all high fashion and wear a garden hose as a belt. I was surprised he didn't look embarrassed by that, but I guess when a device is going to help you *not* suffocate, you don't blush at the thought of it.

"Let's go rob a clown," Walter said, grinning.

Step 1: Break into Twinkles's house

"There he goes!" Kennedy said. We were parked down the street from Twinkles's house, and had been for nearly an hour. I looked up just in time to see a sketchy-looking car swerve away, driven by a man who either had terrible red hair or was wearing an enormous clown wig.

"You're sure?" I asked.

"Of course! Come on!" Kennedy said. Otter and Walter slipped back into the front seat of the car, leaving Kennedy and me to jump in the back. We didn't have anyone running mission control from the farmhouse—everyone there would be too busy at the fake birthday party we were holding to get Twinkles away—which made my ears feel strangely quiet. I wondered if we should have packed two comms just to communicate with one another, in case we somehow became separated—

"That's it," Otter said quietly as he slid the rental car into a street parking spot. He pulled out a map and made a show of opening it as we surveyed the house.

This wasn't going to be easy. The house didn't have much of a backyard, so there wasn't a lot of tree cover. There was a fence, but it was just chain-link, so it wouldn't hide us from the neighbors. We'd need to get inside and out of sight quickly.

The three of us walked slowly up the driveway, at first

acting casual. Then, when we were sure no one was looking, we darted around the side of the house, to the hopefully more secluded backyard—

I groaned. The backyard got brilliant sunlight and was almost entirely consumed by a giant deck. We were practically breaking into this place on a stage. I grabbed ahold of a piece of patio furniture and sat down. Walter and Kennedy plopped into other chairs immediately. Kennedy leaned all the way back in hers, as if enjoying the sun. Anyone who happened to see us would just think we were out enjoying the weather on our porch.

I surveyed the back of the house. Nothing special, except that there was one room just off the deck with a window air-conditioning unit. I removed one of Ben's inventions from my belt—the BENchwarmer—which was basically a pocket-size battering ram. I extended the BENchwarmer—it looked like one of those toy swords, the kind that zips out—then leaned over the deck railing and lined the BENchwarmer up with the air-conditioning unit.

Bang. The BENchwarmer knocked the unit cleanly into the house, leaving a rectangle about one foot by two feet wide open. Before I could even put the BENchwarmer down, Kennedy had sprung over the side of the deck, balancing herself on first the ledge of the deck, then the windowsill. She pushed off the deck and, without the slightest wobble in balance, slid neatly through the window. I went back to looking casual but held my breath; from the looks of it, Walter was holding his too. What if we'd been wrong, and Twinkles was still home? What if—

"Welcome," Kennedy said smartly as she opened the back door, grinning. Walter and I exhaled at once and then hurried in.

I sort of wished we hadn't. Twinkles's house smelled like cheese. I made a face.

"I know. I think it's the trash," Kennedy said, frowning. She didn't mean the trash in the trash can. She meant the trash *everywhere*. The coffee table was covered in food takeout boxes. The floor was covered in laundry—some of it old and dingy underwear, which I knew I'd never be able to unsee. The kitchen was flooded with dirty dishes.

The place was flat-out disgusting.

"This doesn't look like the house of a guy who's carefully keeping thousand-year-old jeweled manuscripts," Walter said warily.

He was right. My stomach felt pitted, but we couldn't give up yet.

Step 2: Find the helium chamber

If there was a helium chamber. As we picked our way through the house, my hope fizzled. It *had* to be here. It had to be here somewhere. Beatrix said he was getting a crazy amount of helium delivered. Yes, he was a clown, but from the photos we saw online, he wasn't a clown many people would hire. He was there the day—

Stop! I shouted to myself. Doubting yourself was a quick way to get burned. At SRS, they always told us to make a decision and stick with it. This was my decision. I had to . . .

"Oh, gross," Kennedy said, gagging as she made her way out of the bathroom.

"Where *is it?*" Walter said, growing frustrated. We'd gone through the entire place, and nothing . . .

"The tanks. He's getting the helium delivered in tanks, and we haven't even seen *those*. We're missing something," I said. I closed my eyes, tried to remember what the exterior of the house looked like. Was there a room visible from the outside that we hadn't gone through inside? I turned the mental picture of the house into a blueprint, traced my way around . . .

"The crawl space," I said, turning to them. "There's probably a crawl space underneath the house. The deck was raised, remember, and the yard was steep? But there's no real basement."

"Million-dollar books in a crawl space. Classy, Twinkles," Walter said, but he looked excited. After a quick glance to make sure neighbors weren't watching, we walked out the back door and over the side of the deck railing (Kennedy and Walter dropped neatly into crouches, while I basically hit the ground and rolled like a log). I went first under the deck. There was *almost* enough room to stand, but not quite. Sunlight peered through the deck slats above us, giving us just enough light to see a very small door—a few feet tall and wide at the most.

There was a fat lock on it, but the door itself was made of flimsy plywood. Since no one could see us under there, Walter karate-kicked the door; it buckled beneath his foot. He stepped aside so I could look in.

Automatic lights flickered on, and cool air rushed out. I gasped.

This room was flawless. Neat, pale gray, and perfectly empty except for a series of helium tanks off to one side, and in the very back, a box that had to be the helium chamber.

We'd found the Runanko books.

CHAPTER SEVENTEEN

"Hale? What do you see?" Kennedy asked urgently. I spun around to her and Walter; they instantly read my expression and grinned. They then shouldered around me to get a look for themselves.

"Whoa," Walter said. "Now, that's what I call a crawl space."

"There they are!" Kennedy said at the same time. "I *knew* Mom and Dad weren't art thieves!" It was strangely relieving to hear Kennedy as pleased as I was about this. She jumped up, nearly hit her head on the ceiling, and then hugged me.

"Guys. *Now, that's what I call a crawl space,*" Walter repeated, motioning to the room.

"Right," I said as Kennedy released me. The room— for all its smooth walls and hissing helium pumps and fanciness—was only about three feet tall. Which meant none of us could safely detach the helium pump from the chamber, because it would flood the room with helium and there'd be no staying low enough to breathe only oxygen-rich air.

"Ideas?" Walter asked, looking grim.

I checked my watch—we'd been at the house for nearly a half hour now. We weren't over time yet, but I wanted to be gone before the full hour was up. I paced in front of the door for a moment, trying to shake the happiness about my parents not being thieves out of my head. *Focus on the mission, Hale.*

"All right," I said, looking at the helium chamber in the back of the crawl space. It was at least ten feet away. "I need a hose. A garden hose."

"I'll find one," Kennedy said immediately, and darted out from under the house. She returned less than a minute later with a long, dirty garden hose slung over her shoulder. "It's the neighbor's," she explained. I withdrew the BEN of All Trades's knife and sliced a seven- or eight-foot section of hose off. "Walter, give me the B(reathe)-EN. Good, now, hold this section, and—Kennedy, hand me the duct tape off my belt. Perfect."

I'd removed the scuba mask from the B(reathe)-EN and extended the tube length by adding the section of hose. It was now long enough to reach the back wall and, if the pump stayed outside, would still provide the mask-wearer clean oxygen.

Walter pulled his shirt off so he was down to just the SRS uniform. He clamped the mask over his mouth and, with a quick look at me and Kennedy, made his way into the crawl space. He couldn't even move on his hands and knees—he had to army crawl along the floor. It really *was* a genius hiding spot. Who would think to look in such a small space for priceless jeweled books? Yet here was the chamber, the helium, the . . .

"How do you think Twinkles made all this?" Kennedy asked quietly as Walter's feet got farther away.

"Maybe he's really clever. Ben could make this," I said.

Kennedy looked doubtful, but we didn't have a chance to discuss it, because Walter shouted over his shoulder.

"Looks like there's a melting lock on the chamber! Probably easiest to just break the glass case!"

"Do it!" I answered.

A few moments later I heard the glass shatter—which meant the air in the crawl space was now filling with helium. I held the oxygen pump as far away from the crawl space entrance as I could so there was no chance it would suck in any helium air. I couldn't see the helium chamber anymore because of Walter's body, and I worried that the pump wasn't making much noise—was it working? Walter was rustling around, moving . . .

He started backing up, emerging from the crawl space. Without the chamber. He rose up, removed the mask, and shook his head.

"I can't get the books out. There's a plinth alarm underneath that I could disarm, but I think there's also some sort of alarm on the back of the chamber. I can't tell what it is, so I'm afraid to unhook it."

I pressed my lips together. Who did the alarms call? A security company? Twinkles himself? "All right—I'll go in and unhook the alarm in the back. Then you go *back* in and undo the pressure alarm, and—"

A car revved, loudly, down by the street. Otter's alarm. Something was wrong—

"Let's go," Walter said frantically.

"No, no—we're here, let's just— Come on, we'll go in together and just trade off the mask. Kennedy, go get in the car," I said hurriedly, stripping down to my SRS uniform.

"No way am I leaving," she said, folding her arms.

I scowled at her, but there was no time to argue. Walter handed over the mask and offered me a leg up—the step into the crawl space was a little high for me, unlike for him. I ducked in and tried to control my breath as the closeness of the ceiling hit me. I slid to one side so that Walter could get in behind me, and then I held my breath so I could hand him the mask. He took a few breaths, traded the mask back to me, and then we crawled toward the helium chamber. There were footsteps above us—someone was in the house. How was Twinkles back already? I glanced at my watch as I handed Walter the mask. We should've had another hour at the least. If he noticed someone broke in, he'd almost certainly come check the books—

I tried to crawl faster, but it was hard, what with holding my breath, the tiny space, and the bits of glass that now littered the floor.

Walter handed the mask back as we got to the chamber. The books were inside, glittering and sparkly, with flecks of broken glass all over them. I held my breath and gave the mask back, then pressed my cheek against the ground to look at the alarm under the chamber—the plinth. This one was simple enough; as long as the button the chamber rested on didn't pop up, it wouldn't go off. It was easy enough to trick with a piece of tape to hold the button down. I wiggled forward to look at the one on the back, and sighed, which meant Walter had to immediately hand me the mask so I could take a breath.

"Pressure alarm. Cushioned," I said before taking a breath of oxygen. I handed it back as Walter's face fell.

Pressure alarms were similar to plinth alarms, only instead of a button that pops up, they required that the pressure on the object remain the same. They're not *impossible* to fool—just tricky. But when they're cushioned . . . well. Think of a bowling ball on a pillow. You lift the ball up, and the pillow will start to fluff back up instantly.

More footsteps upstairs. I heard the car rev again. There was no time to fool the pressure alarm. We had to run for it. Even *I* could outrun an old clown, right? I took the mask back and breathed.

"Take them and run," I whispered.

"What?" Walter asked, his eyes wide, but I was already mouthing, *One, two, three—*

Walter winced as he yanked the books off the platform and hugged them to his chest. The pressure alarm clicked off and began to scream as Walter shimmied backward to the door, unable to use his hands. I braced my feet against his shoulders and pushed him, hard, so he slid most of the way out. The alarm was making my ears ring, and I couldn't hear the footsteps, if Twinkles was coming, if he was yelling.

By the time I got out the door, Walter had the chamber lifted and pressed against his chest. Shadows appeared in the strips of sunlight caused by the deck boards—someone was above, running down. Kennedy and Walter cut to the right, away from the stairs, and were nearly out of sight. I opened my mouth—I could distract Twinkles while they ran for it.

"Hurry! Give the books to me!" I roared, like I was still mid-robbery. Only, my voice wasn't a roar. My voice sounded like a cartoon animal. Stupid helium. I yelled again anyhow, sounding like the most precious burglar in existence. A foot in a cherry-red shoe appeared on the stairs—Twinkles was falling for it.

But then, no. He must have seen Kennedy and Walter, because suddenly he went back up; the shadow was running across the deck. I sprinted out from under it, gasping for non-helium air and squinting in the bright sunlight. Kennedy and Walter were in the side yard, backing up toward the deck as Twinkles—who looked really, really scary at the moment—stalked toward them, shouting in German. Did he have a weapon? I couldn't tell—

An engine revved, tires squealed, and suddenly a car burst over the edge of the driveway, right at Twinkles. It was Otter, his face red and eyes narrowed. Twinkles leaped out of the way just in time to avoid becoming road kill—he was spry for a guy who looked as roughed-up as he did. This gave Kennedy and Walter the time they needed. Otter leaned over and opened the passenger-side door. Walter chucked the books in and then jumped in himself, while Kennedy grabbed for the back door. I ran for the car, unsure if there was enough time for me to make it, but I was relieved to know that unlike my friends, Otter *would* leave me here.

"Steve?" Twinkles said.

Everyone froze. Except Twinkles, whose hands slackened out of fists. He tilted his head to the side. "Steve? Steve Otter?"

I always thought that Otter, for all his arrogance, had probably been a sort of crappy field agent. I mean, great field agents don't get retired and stuck teaching year-six SRS classes, right? But in this moment, Otter's years of spy training kicked in a *thousand* times faster than mine, Walter's, or Kennedy's. He smiled brightly—

"Kevin!"

Twinkles started to smile but then forced his lips back into a straight line. "The tune?"

Without hesitation, Otter whistled a short melody. I had no idea if it was right or not—or how Otter would know it—but Twinkles grinned.

"What's going on?" he asked.

"We needed the books back, and you weren't here," Otter said warmly. "Thought it'd be a nice, easy smash-and-grab mission for my junior agents. Walter, Hale, Kennedy—you have the honor of meeting Kevin Stroganoff. One of SRS's finest deep-cover agents."

CHAPTER EIGHTEEN

Twinkles the Clown was the Runanko book thief. He was also Kevin Stroganoff. He was also, apparently, an SRS agent.

The guy had a lot of identities.

Otter turned and smiled at me flawlessly, but I read the urgency in his eyes: I had to move, or Twinkles was going to know something was amiss. I strode forward and extended my hand and then shook his sharply.

"It's an honor to meet you, sir."

"Honor? Ha. I bet you'd never heard of me before you got to Geneva!" Twinkles said. Kennedy and Walter climbed out of the car, smiles plastered on their faces.

"Not your name, since it's a gold-level mission, but I assure you, everyone's heard of the deep-cover agent in Switzerland," Otter said. He was brief, but in that sentence he told the three of us exactly what story we were to play along with, and the exact truth of the situation: Twinkles had been in deep cover for a very long time. So long that he didn't know everyone in his presence had ditched SRS.

"Gold-level?" Twinkles asked, his eyes shining a bit. He blushed right through his white face makeup. "I didn't know it was elevated to gold-level!"

Otter looked taken aback. "Really? Wow, you *are* in deep cover. I admire it, Kevin, I really do. Takes a certain type of agent to maintain deep cover this long."

"What about you, Steve? What have you—" Twinkles looked down at his clown costume. The armpits were soaked through with sweat stains, and the whole thing had a faded, flappy sort of look to it. "Come on in. Let me change and wash all this makeup off. I'll get everyone some coffee. I was on my way to a party, you know—SRS set me up in the whole clown cover and told me to keep it up. But god, I'm tired of the act. You know I still can't juggle?" He said this as he climbed the stairs up the deck and to the house. Otter hurried to walk beside him. I made eyes at Kennedy and Walter; they understood my instructions and went about quietly moving the helium chamber, with the books still inside, to the trunk of the car, so the oxygen-filled air wouldn't eat away at them. I went on in with Twinkles and Otter in the meantime.

"Anyway, I was on my way to some kid's birthday party on a horse farm or something, when I realized I'd forgotten my balloons." Twinkles stopped in his kitchen and reached between a stack of dirty plates and a row of empty cereal boxes, where he found a bag of long skinny balloons. "We must have just missed each other!"

"Indeed! You know I don't have long to catch up— we've got an exit flight in a few hours. But how have you been? Last I saw you was, what? We were eighteen, maybe? Nineteen?"

"I was nineteen, I think, because I'd only *just* learned Romansh when they sent me here. Remember, they had me doing that undercover elephant trainer work out by the border? You were there for a little while too, I think."

Otter nodded. "Yes, of course! Right, and there was that—"

"Massive power outage!" they said at the same time.

I smiled. Twinkles dumped some instant coffee into five mugs and swirled it around with his paint-stained finger to mix it. Not gagging as I sipped it was one of the more impressive acting jobs of my life, if you ask me.

"What've you been up to? How's the old gang? Most of them still alive?" Twinkles said lightly.

"Oh, sure. I'm teaching now—that's why I'm running around with junior agents. Liz Hartman is teaching too. Will Green is in deep cover in Russia, now, I think."

"What about Katie Mercutio?" Twinkles said, ushering us to his living room. He shoved a load of dirty laundry off a recliner and sat down, crossing his legs so that his giant clown shoes bobbled in front of him.

"Katie Mercutio married Joseph Jordan, actually! They're great—in and out field agents, never undercover for long," Otter said casually. I nodded, doing my best to look a little bored, when in reality my stomach was spinning around, bouncing off my rib cage. They were talking about my parents.

Twinkles nodded knowingly. "Well, then—what all did you need? The Runanko books, obviously, but did you come for the rest? I can help you load it, and we'll have time to eat dinner together! I can make schnitzel!"

"Just the books, actually, though they did ask me to check on the rest of it—make sure it's been cataloged correctly and all," Otter lied smoothly.

Twinkles scoffed. "As if I have anything better to do. The paintings are all upstairs in the attic, temperature controlled. A few others are actually behind the drywall over there"—he nodded to the exterior wall—"in alcoves. SRS finally looking to sell it, now that it's been a while and the hunt for it's cooled off?"

"Exactly," Otter said, and set his coffee down on an end table. "And sure, come on—let's load up, and we'll get . . . uh . . . schnitzel."

"Perfect!" Twinkles rose, kicked off his clown shoes, and made his way upstairs, I assumed to the attic. Otter followed, then me, then Kennedy and Walter, who'd finished transferring the books from the chamber to the helium tank in the trunk. They let their guards down long enough to give me baffled looks; I shrugged. This was weirding me out too.

At the top of the stairs, Twinkles grabbed ahold of a cord and pulled down the attic steps. Rather than leading straight into the attic, however, they led to a sliding steel door. Twinkles put a key in the door but didn't turn it—he didn't need to. The steel panel slid open with an electric whoosh, taking his key with it, revealing lights just like those in the crawl space downstairs.

"Why keep the books downstairs and the art up here?" Otter asked.

Twinkles blanched a little. "I . . . well. I can't carry those helium tanks up the attic stairs anymore. But I swear, the crawl space is perfect! I sealed it—there's no way a rat can get in there! Can you leave that out of your report, please?"

Otter sighed. "Fine. Fine."

Twinkles grinned. "Whew. Anyway—do you have a checklist? I might have one, somewhere. I don't really know who it's by. Not my style, you know?"

"Yep, my junior agents are getting it out of the car now," Otter said warmly.

Twinkles answered as we followed him up the steps. "I'm surprised they didn't send Katie and Joseph to get all this, actually, after they worked so hard to steal it."

There.

It was dropped in so easily, so simply, just another bit of conversation. Twinkles didn't even look back as he climbed the staircase into the attic, which glowed the same mechanical, fluorescent color as the crawl space under the house.

But there it was.

My parents were art thieves, just like Otter had said. But . . .

"Did they steal the Runanko books?" I called up to him. It was stupid—a personal question, unrelated to the mission. Otter dropped his charming cover long enough to glare at me for a split second, but I didn't care. I didn't care about anything right now, except for the answer.

"Of course!" Twinkles said, his voice faraway as he began clanging around above me. "That was our deal— I'd case the place, and they'd rob it. The three of us were never really a team though. It was always *them* and *me*, you know? I guess I shouldn't be surprised they got married. Can't help but admire . . ."

He kept talking, but I wasn't listening. My parents stole the books. They stole art. Otter was right. I was wrong.

How did Otter know more about my parents than I did?

It felt like something was crushing me, but it wasn't shame or anger or anything like that. I felt so . . . stupid.

I just felt stupid.

Twinkles was still talking quickly, but he cut himself off when Otter reached out to touch one of the paintings. "Watch out, Steve! I'll need to disable the power up here. If you try to take them off the walls, the door down there seals us in. Theft prevention, you know. SRS had to come free me three times my first few years here."

Down the street, tires squealed. Once, twice—they were getting closer, the shrill sound louder and louder. "Who's that?" Twinkles said. Otter tensed and then hurried up the steps into the attic. I followed, while Kennedy and Walter went to look out one of the second-floor windows.

I tried not to gape at the art—beautiful, fancy art, the sort you see in textbooks, lined the walls—and instead rushed to join Twinkles and Otter at the round attic window. The two of them were blocking my view.

"Did you forget to turn the alarms off?" Twinkles said, frowning.

"Must have," Otter answered, and despite all his skill, all his training, his voice had dropped and gone flat. He stepped aside so I could see why.

Running up the drive was a team of SRS agents.

Which was pretty bad.

But worse? One of them was Walter's mom.

CHAPTER NINETEEN

Otter punched Twinkles in the head.

I'm not usually a big fan of resorting to punching some-one in the head, because 1) I throw a lousy punch and 2) I wouldn't want to be punched in the head, so I try not to do it to other people. But I knew without asking that this was the best choice—not only because it kept Twinkles from helping SRS capture us, but because it meant that Twinkles had a solid alibi when SRS asked why he *didn't* stop us faster.

Twinkles fell down in a clown-colored heap.

"Get out!" Otter bellowed down to Kennedy and Walter just as Twinkles hit the ground.

"Back is still clear! Walter, *come on!*" Kennedy shouted. The front door burst open in a clattering of wood and metal. Feet raced around downstairs as the SRS agents—five of them, I'd counted—poured inside. Otter and I crept the rest of the way downstairs, using SRS's noise to cover the sound of our own feet. Kennedy and Walter were in what had to be Twinkles's bedroom; Kennedy's eyes were wide and alert, while Walter looked pale.

"Side window," I whispered. Downstairs, SRS agents were shouting to one another—they ran out the back to the crawl space. *So that's who the alarms called,* I thought, hating myself for not considering this. For not believing SRS—or my parents—could be involved. For being so . . .

"Go," Otter hissed. Kennedy sprang down the upstairs hall where there was a small window that overlooked the driveway. Otter grabbed Walter and lugged him that way, while I yanked one of Ben's inventions—the CariBENer—off my belt. Kennedy slid the window open as quietly as possible, while I rigged the CariBENer to . . .

"There's nothing to brace it with," I whispered. "One of us has to hold it."

It couldn't be Kennedy, of course, and Walter looked too disoriented to be useful. I handed the end of the CariBENer to Kennedy and pulled the other end over my shoulder, then sat with my back to the windowpane to brace myself. Kennedy was trembling a little, but only just. She ducked out the window, checked to make sure she could get down without the SRS agents seeing, and then dropped. I winced as the cord from the CariBENer dug into my shoulder. Then I heard the slight clip of my sister's feet hitting the ground, and the pressure on the CariBENer released. The cord zipped back to the window.

"Let me go next—both you and Walter can brace me," Otter said, clipping the CariBENer onto his uniform belt. I nodded—this was almost certainly going to be a getaway chase kind of situation, and Otter was the best driver between us. I wanted him behind the wheel to get my sister and the Runanko books out of here. I wrestled Walter over to me, and between the two of us, Otter made it safely to the ground.

"My mom is downstairs," Walter said faintly as the line zipped back up. I grimaced. I couldn't support Walter's weight, and even though he could likely support mine, I couldn't just leave him here like this—they'd capture him for sure, and I was certain his mother's presence wouldn't make the whole captured-and-hauled-away experience any more comfortable for him.

"Come on," I said, grabbing ahold of his arm. I heard the car rev, and Otter squealed out of the driveway, making way more noise than was necessary—getting the SRS agents' attention. I saw a couple run around the side of the house, weapons drawn—we had a few moments before the remaining agents raced upstairs to check on the art in the attic. I heard a motorcycle or two zip away, agents giving chase, and then more shouting.

The front door. We might be able to make it to the front door, and if we could just get a few houses down, we could hide for at least a little while and then maybe steal a car to get away. *Focus, Hale.* I hurried to the stairs, then down them. Walter was slow, moving at half speed behind me, and he kept stalling at the windows, hoping to get another look at his mom—but giving the SRS agents outside time to spot *us* as well. We were almost to the front door when the back opened.

I shoved Walter into the hall closet and shut the door behind us. It wasn't really the time to be judgmental, but oh my god, the collection of coats in the closet smelled like a giant animal form of Twinkles—a yak, maybe, or a highland cow. I tried to breathe through my mouth as I waited for the sound of the agents moving upstairs.

"Kitchen is clear! Living room clear!" Walter's mom shouted. Did she know it was *us* who'd set off the alarm, or just that it'd been set off? I glanced at Walter and saw his chin wobbling, saw that he was wondering the same thing.

"They're gone. They've got the books that were downstairs. Command, can you send us a resource list of the art that's supposed to be upstairs so we can account for it?" asked another agent, one with a Spanish accent. I heard Mrs. Quaddlebaum sigh, then more feet on the stairs, someone calling Twinkles's name.

I leaned my head out the closet door and then jerked it back in. Just like SRS protocol dictated, they'd left an agent on the ground floor. It was a man; I suspected it was the one with the Spanish accent. He was pacing around, insulting Twinkles's place under his breath.

"Is she upstairs alone? Maybe I can go talk to her," Walter asked. "Please, Hale. I haven't seen her. She won't turn me in."

"She will, and you know it. She's an SRS agent," I said.

"She's my mom!" Walter said, this time a bit too loud. I grimaced as the Spanish man's pacing stopped. He'd heard us. Walter didn't seem to realize he'd caused this, and he kept talking. "Hale, you go. I'll figure something out—"

I clamped a hand down over his mouth, but it was too late. Footsteps were coming toward us. I reached for my belt—but I hadn't packed much onto it, since this was supposed to be a simple break-in, not a showdown with SRS. I reached up and pulled down a coat, something covered in fur that felt like it was about fifty years old. I tugged it on, pulling it up so that my head was covered by it, and then crouched down.

The man grabbed the edge of the door and slowly opened it an inch.

I barked.

And to think, I thought the least dignified thing I'd do this year was get thrown into a pile of garbage bags.

But I barked crazily, growled, and lunged for the door.

The Spanish guy cursed loudly and leaped back, slamming the door shut. "There's a dog down here!" he shouted. "There's a big brown dog! It almost got me!"

"*Did* it get you?" Mrs. Quaddlebaum's voice shot down.

"No!"

"Then stop yelling so we can focus!" she snapped.

The Spanish guy grumbled and said under his breath, "You don't know. It's a really big dog."

That bought us a moment, at least. I shrugged the coat off and then continued to paw and scratch at the door to keep the Spanish guy away. I wondered where Kennedy and Otter were, if they'd managed to throw the motorcycles off their trail. They couldn't get Kennedy; she was the only family I had now . . .

Focus, Hale. I closed my eyes and, slowly, a plan clicked into place.

Mission: Escape without getting
captured/killed/shot at by SRS
Step 1: Electrical malfunction

I pulled the BEN of All Trades off my belt, flicked out the knife, and began quietly cutting into the drywall inside the closet. If I was remembering the house right, I was cutting toward the kitchen—into the wall that the fridge and oven were on. I broke out a piece of drywall, barked again to keep the Spanish guy worried, and looked at my handiwork. Yes—it was the kitchen wall; the pipes and outlets inside the drywall proved it. I shone my flashlight down the wall until I found the outlet the oven used. The oven and dryer were the only things in the house that used enough amps to trip the whole house's breaker.

"Walter. *Walter*," I hissed. He turned to me. "Grab one of the wire hangers. Fold it up on itself so it's just one big twist of wire. About the size of a pencil." Walter, still a little shaky-looking, obeyed as I pried the top off the oven's outlet and rustled around to expose its terminals.

If the house was wired well, this would trip only the oven's circuit.

But given that this was an old house and, from the looks of it, not very well maintained, I didn't think it was wired well. Walter handed me the bent-up coat hanger; I barked again at the door just to be careful.

Then, I counted to myself. *One. Two. Three.*

I released the coat hanger so that it fell flat across the oven's terminals. Sparks sprayed into the wall and back at us, a hiss, a pop, and—

"Hey!" a handful of voices from the attic floated down to us, more muffled than they were before.

"Stop gawking—secure the artwork!" Mrs. Quaddlebaum roared. "Simio! Check the entry points! The emergency door just sealed us in!"

Yes, yes, Mrs. Quaddlebaum was doing everything exactly as SRS had trained her to. She knew the sudden power surge might be intentional, and she knew to send someone to find an intruder before abandoning the artwork she'd come to protect.

I heard Simio run away from us to check the front door, then the back door. "Entry points are clear, Agent Quaddlebaum!"

Despite this, Mrs. Quaddlebaum cursed loudly—Walter looked a little alarmed. "We must have tripped the security on the paintings up here!" she shouted. "Call headquarters and find out the workaround."

"On it!" Simio shouted, and began to hurriedly speak in a lower voice—into his comm, if I had to guess.

"What are we doing?" Walter whispered. I shushed him—I was listening. We only had one shot at this, since I almost certainly couldn't outrun Simio. Any minute now, though . . .

Outside, I heard the squeal of air brakes, as one of Geneva's city buses rolled into the bus stop.

"*Now*," I snapped, and pushed open the closet door. I didn't even look for Simio—instead I charged toward the front door and flung it open hard enough that it nearly bounced back and hit me in the face. Simio was shouting now—he knew something was wrong—but Walter was behind me and the bus was ahead, a hundred feet, seventy-five feet, fifty feet . . .

The driver started to shut the doors—

"*Tenez le bus!*" I shouted. *Hold the bus!* The driver looked up—she saw us. We were going to make it. SRS couldn't chase two kids down onto a public bus without causing a scene! I looked over my shoulder . . .

Walter.

He was frozen a dozen or so feet behind me, staring at the attic window. There was Mrs. Quaddlebaum, shouting words we couldn't hear, her eyes locked on her son, her fists pounding the window. Was she angry or sad? I couldn't tell from here. Walter lifted a hand in a sort of wave, and suddenly his body seemed very small and breakable.

"*Walter!*" I roared. Walter jumped, turned back to me, and then jogged—*jogged, not ran*—to the bus. We jumped on just as Simio reached the top of Twinkles's yard.

"Should I wait for him too?" the driver asked.

"No, no—we're fine. He's just mad we're late for karate," I said, grinning brightly. The bus driver nodded and pulled away, leaving Walter and me to stumble to the back to sit down. I began calculating where and when we'd change buses and how we'd evade SRS until we could make it back to the farmhouse. Walter, however, just looked dazed. I was boiling, my heart pounding, head cloudy with anger.

He could have gotten us caught.

He could have gotten us killed.

"Hale?" Walter said quietly after a moment. I took a breath, prepared what I'd say after he apologized, and prepared in my head to forgive him. Walter continued once I was looking at him. "Do you think my mom was glad to see me, even if it was like this?"

I stared. Walter looked away.

And we rode on in silence.

CHAPTER TWENTY

When we got back to the farmhouse, Clatterbuck and the twins swarmed us. Their faces made that phrase "worried sick" seem like more than just a saying. Even Annabelle was riled up. She met us in the front yard with the others, leaping on each of us—and knocking us to the ground—in turn.

"All right, all right," Otter said, pushing Annabelle's paws off his shoulders. "We'll explain everything. Let's just get inside." Kennedy was already halfway through telling the whole story, and by the time we sat down, she'd made it up to the part about the crawl space. I hadn't said a word. Neither had Walter.

Here's the thing: I didn't necessarily blame Walter, my friend, for freezing when his mom called his name.

But I did sort of blame Walter, my *partner*, for freezing when his mom called his name. I blamed him for being so unable to function when he realized his mom was near that we ended up trapped in that closet to begin with.

Walter was trained better than that. *SRS* trained him better than that. Those sorts of mistakes were the things that cost people their lives.

How was I supposed to trust Walter in the field now? I was able to make up for his mistakes, sure, but would Kennedy have been able to? Would Otter, would the twins or Clatterbuck?

"How did you know the tune code, anyway?" Kennedy asked Otter, her face glowing with excitement.

Otter shrugged, unimpressed with himself. "I just whistled Pachelbel's Canon. It sounds like everything." Clatterbuck's eyes widened with delight, and then he punched at Otter's shoulder like a proud brother. Otter scowled. Clatterbuck punched his shoulder again. Clatterbuck and Annabelle really had a lot in common, I decided.

"Anyway, so, Hale—tell us what happened after we got out," Kennedy said.

"I tripped the circuit to the house using the oven. Then we jumped onto a bus," I said absently.

"The oven? Wow, Hale. That was really bright," Clatterbuck said warmly, though he still looked a little panicked.

"Really bright, and it didn't have to happen," Otter said shortly. He drummed his fingers on the table. "We should never have gone in there like that. We needed time to plan, to really put a mission together—"

"It was supposed to be simple—" I interrupted.

"That's how agents fail, and you know it," Otter answered.

I didn't have a response. Because he was right.

I really, really hate it when Otter is right. First about my parents, now about the mission . . . I shook my head. *Think of the mission, Hale.* I crushed all my feelings back into my chest—I could deal with those another day. "Fine. Fine—the bank, then. Let's plan it out. Really plan it, like we should've planned this one."

"We can't rob a bank now! Not only is SRS in Geneva, we've already been spotted!" Otter said, like I'd lost my mind entirely.

"We can't just *leave*, though," Kennedy said. "What about the books? Hastings? Annabelle?" She grabbed Annabelle's head and hauled it into her lap. "We can't just leave her with Hastings!"

"She's not our dog, Kennedy," I reminded her.

"She doesn't even *like* Hastings. All she did there was lie on the floor. At least she has fun with us," Kennedy said. Annabelle snaked her head over the tabletop and licked up a few crumbs in response.

"Here's the plan," Otter said, folding his arms. "We give the dog back—don't make that face, Kennedy; we have to—we resell the books, and we use the money to fund The League and stop SRS."

Mouths opened. Mine wasn't one of them.

"That's stealing—the books belong to Hastings. And that's what SRS does—what they *did*," Walter said.

"We can't be like them!" Kennedy said at the same time, and then she added, "But if we're going to steal from him, can't we take Annabelle instead of the books?"

She had a point. Beatrix and Ben were mostly quiet, but Clatterbuck stammered something about never wanting to be part of SRS, having been a League agent from the start.

Then they all looked at me. I kept my face calm, my eyes steady. "We see if it's possible to rob the bank, like we planned. But if it *isn't* . . . well. We have to have something to live off, guys. We can't keep going up against SRS with homemade inventions and three kid agents."

"What's wrong with my inventions?" Ben asked, hurt.

"Nothing! Nothing's wrong with them. I'm just saying, SRS is powerful. Money makes them powerful. If we can't take their power away, we have to find a way to build some of our own."

"But we're not like SRS," Kennedy said, crossing her arms.

"We *are*, though. We can't help it. They trained us, Kennedy. Everything we are is because of them. And they're *good* at what they do, evil as it may be. Maybe functioning a little more like they are will get us closer to stopping them."

"Speak for yourself," Walter said shortly. "They've still got my mom. I don't want to be anything like them."

"They don't *have* your mom, Walter. She chose them!" I said, my voice sharp. Walter looked liked I'd struck him; he stepped back, his eyebrows knitted together, his mouth parted. I was instantly sorry and not sorry—sorry to have hurt him, not sorry because of how badly I wanted Walter to realize this for himself. His mom chose SRS.

Just like my parents chose to be art thieves.

Like they chose to leave us.

It wasn't something I wanted to think about, and it definitely wasn't something I could say out loud, but there it was: my parents chose to leave me and Kennedy behind. I'm not saying it was easy, but that was still the choice they made. Maybe sometimes you just have to be like SRS and think of the mission. Maybe sometimes, you have to put aside what feels right or wrong or good or bad and just do what has to be done.

Maybe sometimes, you act like SRS because otherwise, they win again, and you are just so, so, so tired of them winning.

"I don't want to keep the books," I said, trying not to let all the mean thoughts in my head leak into my voice.

"But I also don't want SRS to crush us, and if we don't get a leg up on them, eventually they will. Let's put together a bank plan. See what we can do. We'll get everything perfect, all scenarios covered, and go from there."

Except, I knew that what I was *actually* saying was, *We'll see*, which is what your parents say when they mean, *You're not getting what you want, but I don't want to say no.* Everyone else knew it too.

But no one left, because at SRS, we were taught to never walk away from mission planning.

"I . . . um. I have the bank blueprints?" Beatrix said meekly. She tapped at her Right Hand; a nearby printer buzzed to life and spit out page after page of material. Basic blueprints. Vault information. Alarm systems.

It was overwhelming, especially seeing as how we were all still steaming silently. We passed the papers around the table, staring at them, while Annabelle began to snore in the corner.

Have you ever been stuck? Like, writer's block or painter's block or just one of those times where you read part of a book five times but still don't really know what it says? That was what planning the bank job felt like. Usually, we all clicked into place to form the perfect mission, everyone with their own little roles to play, their own parts in the bigger picture. But tonight? Tonight it was like we were seven strangers, and none of us spoke the same language.

Otter finally sighed heavily. "All right—go to sleep. That's an order, everyone. We'll work on the mission tomorrow. Ben, get the books out of the car, will you, and bring them to my room. Kennedy, sweep the perimeter to make sure we weren't followed. Beatrix, double-check that your uncle's rental cars don't trace to us, just in case SRS is looking."

"What about us?" Walter asked, motioning to me and himself.

"You two, don't talk. Just go to sleep," Otter said.

Which was fine by me. Walter went straight to our room, but I didn't want to have to lie in there, wondering if he was awake. I could feel all sorts of words on the tip of my tongue—*Walter, I can't trust you anymore. Walter, you were useless today, and you're supposed to be my partner. Walter, you have to let your mom go.* It was definitely for the best that we weren't alone, where I might crack and say them. I opted to join Kennedy on the perimeter sweep. I think she knew why I wanted to get out of the house for a little while; she didn't say much as we walked down the drive, along the edge of the pasture. Annabelle came with us, running ahead and bringing back sticks, which instead of giving us to throw, she gnawed into pieces and then abandoned.

We could see the owners' house up ahead, looking warmer and brighter and more lived-in than the farmhouse. The *poneys* were in a barn nearby for the evening, and when the wind blew just right, you could hear them chomping on hay or stamping their feet or generally being ponies. When we got a little closer, we could see the owners inside, sitting in front of their television on a couch so soft, it looked like it was swallowing them. They were old and wrinkly people who looked like they would give good hugs.

"I think what you said to Walter was mean," Kennedy said softly. I turned, realizing she'd fallen a few steps behind me. She had her head down and was kicking a rock along the path. Kennedy argued with me occasionally, but over stupid things—like what time to wake up, or how many unicorn temporary tattoos she could feasibly fit on her arms. This, however, was very different, and so it threw me. I stopped on the path, trying to drum up the arguments I'd shove at Otter or Walter or even Beatrix, but they didn't come.

"He could've cost us our freedom today. He could have cost us our lives, even. If he can't focus in the field, then . . ."

"He just misses his mom."

"Still," I said, stopping and leaning against one of the wooden pasture fences. There were no clouds in the sky, and even with the glow of downtown Geneva's lights a few miles away, you could see a billion stars.

Kennedy kicked her rock again, hard enough that it vanished down the trail. Annabelle took off after it. "I miss Mom and Dad too."

I turned to her. "Of course you do. So do I. I'm not mad at Walter for missing his mom, Kennedy."

"What happens if Mom and Dad appear, and I freeze?" she asked quietly. "Or you? What would you do if you suddenly saw them again?"

I exhaled a deep chesty breath. Behind us, the lights in the farmhouse clicked out as the owners went to bed. It made the already brilliant stars even more so, and the moonlight made the entire world look dark blue. I picked a few splinters from the fence, letting them drop to the ground, and finally said, "All right, that's fair. I might freeze too. And I wouldn't blame you if you did." I smiled a little and stepped down from the fence. "I guess sometimes I just get angry, like today with Walter. Lately it's hard for me to be a regular person instead of an SRS agent. And sometimes it's hard to be an SRS agent instead of a regular person. I don't know why it's hard for me right now. I never had trouble with that when we were actually at SRS."

"That's because there we didn't get to be regular people very often," Kennedy reminded me. "Remember how long it took for me to convince them to let me start a cheerleading squad? And how we couldn't eat what we wanted, and how they wouldn't let you become a junior agent even though you were the best one in your class? They wanted us to be agents, but they didn't much want us to be people."

"Yeah, but . . . I think . . ." I looked at Kennedy for a long time before continuing—did I really want to admit this? "I think the person I am might *be* an SRS agent. I try to be a regular person, but all I can do is think about how SRS would do something, how they'd plan the mission, how they'd question the witnesses . . ."

Kennedy lifted her eyebrows at me. "So you're a spy, Hale. Isn't that what you always wanted to be anyway?"

"Well, yeah, but . . . I don't want to be an *SRS* spy."

Kennedy shook her head. "Stop being dumb. You're not an SRS spy. Like, you couldn't possibly be *less* of an SRS spy. You're working with their enemy, remember?" We rounded the corner; Kennedy did a neat cartwheel and, without missing a beat, added, "And you *love* being a spy, so who cares where you got your start, so long as you're on the good side now? Stuff like taking Annabelle—yeah, Walter and I didn't really like that, but it was something *The League* needed to do to make the mission work, right? Right. You think of the mission, and that's a good thing, even if SRS taught you that."

"I don't want to *always* be thinking of the mission. I don't want to always put it first. I don't want SRS to own me forever. I don't want to be like Mom and Dad," I said, and the words fell out of my mouth before I realized that maybe that wasn't the best thing to say in front of my little sister. I was relieved when Annabelle bounded out of the darkness toward us with Kennedy's rock in her mouth. She dropped it at our feet and looked pleased.

"Good girl, Annabelle," Kennedy said, ruffling the dog's ears. I walked over to do the same, and we listened for a few minutes to the sound of the ponies munching and Annabelle panting.

"I shouldn't have said that about Mom and Dad. I'm sorry," I said when even animal noises couldn't lift the weight between us.

"Don't be sorry. I'm mad at them too," Kennedy said, sighing heavily. "I still miss them. I still love them. I just wish they were here."

I exhaled and then put my arm around Kennedy's shoulders. We continued along the path.

"You know, though, that SRS doesn't really own you, right, Hale?" she asked as we rounded the bottom of the pasture and started back toward the farmhouse.

"I guess," I said.

"They don't. Because if we were at SRS, you wouldn't be worried about any of this stuff. You'd just follow orders."

I looked down at Kennedy and frowned. Then I almost smiled. "I guess you have a point."

She nodded. "That's what makes us different. All of us. And that's when everyone else at SRS will start leaving and joining us—when they can't help but worry about right and wrong and good and bad. They'll join us, and it'll be great because then the whole hall at The League will be full, and we can all pick out a song to wake up to in the morning, like they do at camp."

"Wait, what?"

"At camp? In the movies, when they blast a song over the loudspeaker? It'll be like that," Kennedy said, looking pleased.

"Right. You have to be the one to tell Otter about that plan though," I said, and we finally climbed the steps back up to the farmhouse. Annabelle jumped on Clatterbuck hard enough to knock him over, like she'd missed him horribly while we were gone, and then Kennedy hauled Annabelle off to her bedroom. While I brushed my teeth, I heard Kennedy and Beatrix trying to get Annabelle to leap between the beds without touching the floor. The frequent crashes told me she was no more of an athlete than I was.

Then I went and sat in the kitchen for a moment, looking at Beatrix's equipment and Ben's inventions and the blueprints of the bank and the stack of glasses and plates by the sink from dinner, because if there was one thing every League agent could agree on, it was how gross doing the dishes was.

Back at SRS, my parents did the dishes in the evening, and the cafeteria staff did them at lunch.

Back at SRS, there was a fancy lab for inventions, with sleek electronics and supercomputers.

Back at SRS, I was an agent in training. I was Hale the Whale.

I realized, sitting there and looking at the pile of dirty dishes, that maybe Kennedy was right. Maybe all those things that I was made out of—SRS agent, Hale the Whale, and League agent who hated doing dishes—were just parts of who I was. I was a spy. I was a former SRS agent. I was a current League agent. And I was a hero—or at least, I was trying to be one, and that was something.

But despite all that . . . maybe I needed to be a better friend.

CHAPTER TWENTY-ONE

The next morning, we concluded that we needed as many details as Hastings would give us before coming up with even a loose bank plan. We left the Runanko books in the trunk of the car and opted not to tell Hastings we had them with us, just in case he tried to pull something and get the books without trading us the information. Much to Kennedy's—and, I'll be honest, everyone else's—dismay, we'd brought Annabelle with us to give her back to Hastings.

"You have the books? Really? You really, really have them?" Hastings asked, his eyes globelike with surprise and wonder. He totally ignored Annabelle, who looked around heavily at her former home, then slumped onto the floor, like the very building zapped her energy. Ben and Kennedy sat down with her and petted her quietly, I think secretly hoping that if they laid low, Hastings would forget about Annabelle entirely and we'd be able to take her back with us.

I said, "We do. They were stolen by SRS, as it turns out. That clown that came over was a deep-cover agent."

Hastings shook his head. "Wait—SRS has the books? *And* they're blackmailing me? And their agents are *clowns*?"

"The two situations might not even be related. The books were stolen long before you started working at the bank—long before you inherited your grandmother's possessions. SRS was on something of an art theft spree at the time, trying to have a nice stockpile of assets that could be sold or bargained with," Otter said.

"They had the books *and* my secret. That's . . . well, it's genius, frankly," Hastings said, pacing, his face contorted with a sort of impressed anger.

Otter went on, "Well, all this means, Mr. Hastings, that you can have your books, and you can sell them and buy your own private SRS-free island somewhere."

"An island!" Hastings said, his face lighting up. "I could! I could sell this dump and the books and that dog and get an *island*—"

"You're going to sell Annabelle?" Beatrix asked, horrified. She dropped down beside Kennedy and flung her arms around the dog. Annabelle smacked her lips in response.

"Who cares? She's just a fancy mutt anyway! And besides, on my island, I'll have . . . monkeys. Yes! No, cats. Cats are easier than monkeys, aren't they? Maybe no animals. Parrots!" Hastings said in a frenzy of wealth-dreaming glee. I glanced at Walter warily, and he gave me a look that said, *I can't wait to be finished with this guy.*

"Me either," I muttered.

"What?" Hastings asked. I shrugged, and he went on, "So, SRS's account numbers, right?"

"Yes," Otter said. "We want to know where the money is now, and where it's going to be. And I want to know the bank's security procedures."

"Okay . . . ," Hastings said, wandering toward the living room. He sat down on the couch, Otter took out a legal pad to take notes, and Beatrix held her hand anxiously over her Right Hand. "SRS has its money in three places at the bank. A third of it is in gold bars. A third of it is in cash. And a third is just digital, really—not sitting in a vault anywhere. That's the money they use for day-to-day operations."

Otter nodded. "All right—and who decides where the money goes?"

"I do, mostly. Every now and then they'll ask me to do something specific with it—put it all in an account here or there—but I think that's usually when they're trying to fool a background check. They can make people appear to be millionaires, you know. The digital money is easy to move around. The physical money is trickier. Sometimes it's in private vaults, sometimes safe deposit boxes, and sometimes it's in the main vault with the rest of the cash."

"Shocking," Otter said drily. "So, you could feasibly put it all in one giant private vault for us to rob?"

Hastings frowned. "Well, no. They'd notice if everything was put in one place, I'm sure. I could have the gold moved to . . . to the safe deposit boxes, maybe? It's about thirty million in gold bars. I could spread those out among safe deposit boxes, so it'd all be in the same room. The boxes would be easier to rob."

"All right—what about the cash?" Otter asked.

"The cash is always in either the main vault, which is basically impossible to rob, or in a private vault, which is . . . also impossible to rob. Well—impossible without having an access card." He reached into his pocket and withdrew a card. "Like this one."

Otter smiled dangerously. "Then we'll need you to give that to us."

"It's not that easy—it's the card, plus a retinal scan, plus a guard will check the weight of everyone going in and out of the vault to make sure it hasn't increased. No one's allowed back there but bank employees, and the guards know us all by name. Unless you're planning to go in with a gun, you can't get into that vault. *But* . . . I can go in. I can go get the money for you."

"Why would you do that?" I asked, lifting an eyebrow. So far I'd seen Hastings commit exactly zero selfless acts, and he had to know we couldn't afford to pay him . . . "Ah, you want a cut of the money."

"No," Otter said. "Not a chance. You've gotten your reward, Hastings. You have your books back. How could you possibly need yet more money?"

"Fine, fine," Hastings grumbled. "You'll never get into the vault though. Even with my help, you'd need SRS to call and authorize me to move that amount of money from the vault."

I glanced at Beatrix, who nodded quickly. She could fake the authorization, but . . . Hastings was right. The vault would be tricky.

Otter went on, "Anyway—the digital money?"

"I guess you could do a massive withdrawal and get it in cash? But no, that wouldn't work—there's actually not enough cash in the bank on a given day to cover that amount."

"What if we moved it to another digital account? An account *we* own?" I asked.

Hastings considered this. "That would work. Though the bank might get suspicious—it's a little suspect for a thirty-million-dollar account to appear out of nowhere. Unless, of course, a banker has cleared it." He smiled again, terribly.

"Mr. Hastings, we're not paying you to help us. You *agreed* to help us in return for the Runanko books," Otter said firmly.

"Well, maybe I didn't know how much work helping you would entail!" Hastings pouted. "What are you going to do with all this money anyway? You also want a private island?" Hastings asked, looking between the seven of us.

"That's up for some debate," I said.

"Space camp!" Ben said brightly.

"You mean like . . . *in* space? Because this is a lot of money," Hastings said.

I smiled politely. "We're going to use it to do good. SRS has done a lot of bad, and we want to undo it."

"All right, all right . . . ," Hastings said. But he was fidgeting, which wasn't a good sign. Hastings was starting to realize how plausible it was for us to rob a bank—and how plausible it was for him to either get in on it or get in our way.

"How much do you want?" I asked suddenly. Everyone turned to look at me, surprised. I repeated the question, and added, "You help us get the cash out. What's your cut?"

"*Now* you sound like bank robbers!" Hastings said in a voice that delighted him and depressed me. All this time hoping my parents weren't thieves, and here I was becoming one. "Forty percent," Hastings said.

"No," Otter and I answered immediately.

Hastings shrugged. "Well, you can maybe rob the bank on your own. But if you've already stolen the books from SRS, I bet they'll be on the lookout for you—so getting in without my help would be hard. In fact, I hope no one *tips SRS off* about your plans—"

Otter was across the room, one fist raised to Hastings, before I even realized what was happening. For an older guy, he could really move. He had Hastings's collar in one hand, using it to pull the man closer to his face. Otter's teeth were bared, and his eyes were lit up.

"Are you threatening us, Mr. Hastings? After all we've done for you? After we returned what SRS stole?" Otter hissed.

Clatterbuck cleared his throat, like he thought perhaps he should intervene, but then he didn't. Violence wasn't really The League's *thing*, but I wasn't particularly sad about seeing Hastings roughed up.

Hastings coughed and flailed his arms a bit until Otter released him and took a step back; Otter's nostrils were flared like a bull's. "No, no," Hastings said, scrambling back into a chair. "No. Of course not."

"Excellent. In that case, we'll be in touch for the various account numbers. You'll need to get to work making sure all those accounts are open and working smoothly. Ah, and the safe deposit boxes—we'll need those numbers too," Otter said shortly, turning to walk away.

"Wait! When do I get my books?" Hastings called out.

"When we have the account numbers," Otter said, then to the rest of us, added, "Let's go, everyone. We've got to figure out how to rob a bank."

We rose and moved to the door, and Annabelle started to follow us. When Kennedy told her to "sit" and "stay," the dog looked alarmed and then let out a heartbreaking, low whine. Even Otter flinched.

"It'll be okay, Kennedy. Come on," Beatrix said quietly. Kennedy's eyes were big and watery; I moved so she could be first out the front door and cry without Hastings hearing. I made the mistake of looking back at Annabelle as I rounded up the end of our line. She was lying with her giant head in her paws, ears up and brows knitted together worriedly. And she was drooling, but even though I *knew* it was drool, it still looked like she was actually lying in a puddle of tears.

"She likes cheese," I said to Hastings, shaking my head at him.

"What? The dog? Look—forty percent. Just remember I offered!" Hastings said.

"We don't need your help," I called back, then slammed the door.

At least, I hoped we didn't need his help. Remember when I said that terrified people are the most dangerous? I take that back. Greedy people were the most dangerous. They wanted *more*, no matter what it was, no matter who got hurt. *More, more, more.* What was scarier than some-one willing to work for a secret crime organization so he could get *more*?

And Hastings was basically the greediest person I'd ever met.

CHAPTER TWENTY-TWO

Here is what we had:
5 kids
2 adults
1 rental car (slow, crappy)
1 inside man (untrustworthy)

Here is what the bank had:
Laser grids
Digital cameras
Underground sensors
21-inch-thick vault doors
Armed guards

Here is what SRS had:
The jump on us

I'd actually written all that out just so I could visualize it better. I was starting to regret doing that, since I basically went from 80 percent grim to 98 percent grim before midnight. Everyone else had gone to bed ages ago, but I knew I'd just lie in the bottom bunk, awake. There had to be a way. We had to make this work.

But my head kept going in the exact opposite direction I wanted. When I couldn't immediately sort out how The League could *rob* SRS, I started thinking of the many ways SRS could . . . well. Destroy us, basically. They could show up during the robbery. They could slip a GPS on us and swarm us later on, when there were no witnesses. They could move all their money early, then let us get caught by the Swiss government and thrown in jail.

They had countless options. We had none.

Of course, it was possible we could get in and out of the bank without SRS knowing, but I doubted it. Now that they knew we were in Geneva, they were probably watching all their assets here—from their agents to their cars to their money—very closely. If we so much as sneezed in public, they would come running with a tissue. And by "tissue," I meant a pair of carbon steel handcuffs. Plus, I wasn't so sure Hastings wasn't planning to tip them off. He didn't seem like the sort of guy who would suddenly start helping us for "the greater good."

A door down the hall opened; I recognized the footsteps as Kennedy's immediately. She was wearing fuzzy socks, like she always did in bed, and pajamas with uni-corns on them.

"Did I wake you up?" I asked, my voice low.

Kennedy shook her head. "I woke up a half hour ago and haven't been able to go back to sleep. Is there a plan yet?" She sat down on one of the kitchen chairs and tucked her knees up into her pajama top, eyes cast down toward the blueprints.

"No," I admitted. "I think . . . I think we're done here, Kennedy."

"What? No!" Kennedy said.

"If it's not safe to go in, we're not going in. SRS responded pretty quickly to the alarm at Twinkles's, and we *still* got away. You know how they are—they'll do *any-thing* to make sure they catch us if the opportunity pops up again. You know what they always say—"

"'No amount of firearms can turn a bad mission into a good one,'" Kennedy said glumly.

"Well, actually, I meant, 'Assume the worst will hap-pen.' And there are a *lot* of worsts in this mission."

Kennedy sat with me and stared at everything for a lit-tle while, occasionally opening her mouth to share an idea, but then shutting her mouth and shaking her head before she ever made it to words.

"Maybe we should start small. Think about the *easiest* way to get the money out of the bank, then build up to actually *robbing* it," Kennedy said. This was an SRS exercise, designed to keep agents from overcomplicating things.

"All right. Easiest way to get money out of the bank is to go to the teller, hand them ID, and take it," I said.

"Right. Except, that won't work, because we're taking out way, way more than the daily limit, and because if anyone uses Antonio Halfred's ID, it'd tip SRS off," Kennedy said.

I smiled at her—we'd never really planned a mission together before. I thought about telling her how she looked like Dad when she was thinking hard, but instead I said, "So in that case, let's break it down. There's the digital account, the gold, and the cash."

"Let's start with the gold. Hastings said he could put it in safe deposit boxes, right?" Kennedy said.

Another door down the hall opened—the one to my room. Walter came out, stumbling a little and rubbing his eyes. His hair was sticking up all over and didn't lie flat even after he patted it down. "You guys planning?" he asked, his voice gravelly with sleep.

"Trying to," I said. "We're at the gold in the safe deposit boxes. Trying to sort out the easiest way first."

Walter rubbed his nose and sat down beside Kennedy. "Well, easiest way to get into a safe deposit box is to have the key. Second easiest way though is to have your own box in the same room so you have a legitimate reason to be in there, opening stuff. Then once you're there, you pop the lock on the other box and *boom*."

"Explosions?" Kennedy asked eagerly.

"Huh? No. *Boom*, you're into the safe deposit box," Walter clarified. Kennedy's face fell.

"Except, we don't need to steal something from one safe deposit box. We need to get it from twenty or thirty," I said. I pointed to the blueprints. "There are cameras in the safe deposit room. They'll notice if we're suddenly picking through thirty boxes."

"Plus, even if they don't, they'll notice when we try to walk out with all that gold. It'll be heavy—we'll need some sort of equipment to move it," Walter said.

"How much gold is it, exactly? How big is thirty million dollars worth of gold?" Kennedy asked.

"One thousand, five hundred pounds," another voice said from down the hall. Ben, yawning and pattering toward us.

"Did we wake you up?" Kennedy asked.

"No, I think Walter did—did you know you snore, man?" Walter glowered at Ben.

"Anyway," Ben went on, "there're probably about fifty-six or fifty-seven gold bars. They weigh around twenty-seven pounds each. So, one thousand, five hundred pounds of gold. Three-quarters of a ton."

"We can't just carry that out the front door," I said, shaking my head. "We'd need equipment. A vehicle that can carry that kind of weight."

"I could probably fit one of the cars, but it'd take a few days, at least," Ben said.

"Even if I help you?" Beatrix asked. Her nightshirt was on inside out, but she didn't seem to care. She stopped by the refrigerator to get a can of soda before joining us at the table.

"Even if you help me," Ben said, after thinking for a moment, "welding just takes time, is all."

I dropped my head. "Okay. Let's table the gold for now. The digital money—Beatrix, can you handle that?"

Beatrix winced. "Well . . . sort of."

We blinked.

"The bank runs on a very secure encrypted network, not entirely unlike the SRS facility back home did. So, I can break into the accounts, but I'll have to do it from inside the building, using its own network. But I think Hastings is right—without some sort of prior approval, the bank will know something's up when a thirty-million-dollar account appears out of nowhere. The security system will allow them to pinpoint my location within the building."

"How long would you have before they realized what you were doing and where you were?"

"Long enough to get the money out of the accounts. Not long enough to move it into a new account for us. And not long enough for me to get *out* of the building. Now, maybe Hastings could do it, since they expect him to be moving money around . . ."

"Without Hastings," Otter said grimly. "I don't trust him. We should never have trusted him. From the start he's been all about money and power and private islands. If he knows anything at all about this heist, I think he'll sell the information to SRS."

"The people who stole his books?" Beatrix asked doubtfully.

"The people who will pay him the most," I corrected. "We wouldn't give Hastings forty percent of the cash, but SRS would—they'd probably pay anything to catch us. In *fact*, if I were SRS, I'd have a special team assigned to us. I'd be combing through satellite footage, looking for us. I'd set up teams all over town, plant agents at the airport . . ." I drifted off. Planning for SRS came so easily. I knew exactly what they'd do, where they'd go, what they'd want. I wondered at how simple it had to be for the agents there—for Mrs. Quaddlebaum. They were probably getting neat little folders with assignments in them, instructions to go to a café and pounce if they saw me come in and order a sandwich.

It was easier for them. It was easier for *me* to think like them.

"What else would you do?" Otter asked carefully.

I looked at him and shrugged. "If I had enough notice, I'd probably quietly move the money out of the bank. Replace the gold with fakes, then wait to capture us when we arrived to steal it."

Otter was staring. His eyes were growing wider.

And suddenly I realized exactly what he was thinking.

I grinned—nervously, but I grinned. "Guys, I think we've got a plan."

CHAPTER TWENTY-THREE

At SRS there are projects, operations, and missions.

The projects are the big things—the overarching stuff that involves a whole bunch of different steps. The operations are a step below that—short-term goals that all lead up to a project. And the missions are small, single-goal endeavors, like stealing the Runanko books or vetting the country club kids.

I'd been on a number of missions, of course, and even *those* were difficult to plan. And yet, we were about to undergo something so complicated, so involved, that there was no way it could all be rolled into one mission.

Operation Vengeance for Annabelle
Mission 1: Steal the gold

Mission 2: Get the cash
Mission 3: Rob the digital accounts

(Kennedy titled the operation—she was really upset about Hastings being all shrug-y about Annabelle's future.)

We returned to Hastings's place the following day to get the account numbers and trade them for his books. Only four of us—me, Otter, Clatterbuck, and Ben—had come this time. Clatterbuck was currently maneuvering a truck around the streets of Geneva with a horse trailer attached, rehearsing his part of the plan. Kennedy and Walter were back at the farmhouse working on some sort of crazy gymnastics toss, along with Beatrix, who was working on the hacking bit of this whole scheme. I'd promised them all that I'd check in on Annabelle, so I called her name.

"Don't bother. I had to lock her up in the bathroom because she wouldn't stop trying to get in my bed. But then she just howled all night," Hastings said. He *did* look satisfyingly sleep-deprived, I realized.

"Kennedy and Beatrix let her sleep in their beds while we had her," Ben explained.

"Great," Hastings muttered. "Just great—hey!"

Annabelle suddenly came bursting into the room, feet sliding on the hardwood floors. Her nails dug for traction, but she crashed into a buffet anyhow, sending its candlesticks flying. Hastings yelled at her, but she didn't notice—she tackled me, then Clatterbuck, then Otter and Ben, and then rotated back to knock me down a second time just for good measure.

"What's all over her fur?" I asked. She was covered in white powder and bits of . . . "Oh," I realized. "It's drywall."

"Drywall?" Hastings said, confused. His face morphed to horrified; he turned and raced through the house. We followed out of curiosity, and when we caught up with him, he was staring at an Annabelle-size hole in the bathroom wall (which is to say, an enormous hole in the bathroom wall).

"She *ate her way* through the wall!" Hastings shouted.

"To get to us!" Ben added, sounding pleased.

"It would seem that way," Otter said. Even *he* looked touched by Annabelle's act of destructive affection. I rubbed Annabelle's ears, and she licked my hand. Hastings tried to balance a particularly large chunk of broken drywall back in its place on the wall; it tumbled to the ground, where he stomped on it angrily.

"Well, come along now, Mr. Hastings—you can worry about bathroom renovations another day," Otter said, waving his hand to stave off the drywall dust. "We need to discuss the bank robbery."

"What about it?" Hastings said, trudging away from the bathroom and casting furious glances at Annabelle.

Otter sighed. "Unfortunately, we do need your help after all. But we're not offering more than thirty percent of the take."

"All right, all right, thirty percent," Hastings said, brightening a bit. "Tell me what you need."

As we reached the kitchen, I withdrew a piece of paper from my pocket. On it we'd outlined Hastings's responsibilities. "It's easy, really. We'll call in a fake authorization for the cash to be moved. All you have to do is roll it to the loading dock. We'll be there with a truck, the same one we're using to transport the gold. The big thing, though, is you have to do this at *exactly* ten o'clock on Tuesday morning. If you come any earlier, we won't be down there to help you load it, and it'll look suspicious."

"Ten o'clock. Got it. What happens if I get there late?"

"Don't," Otter snapped. "We're going to send four agents into the safe deposit room to steal the gold at the same time you're getting the cash. The longer you take, the longer my people have to sit around in the loading docks with thirty million in stolen gold."

"What about the digital money? Did you find a way to get that? Because I could help you with that too for a little more . . . ," Hastings said wickedly.

Otter rolled his eyes. "One of our agents will be in the building lobby and hack the system from there. She'll move the cash into one account. So, yes. If you can set up an account for us that we can drop the money into, that would be useful."

"What do I get for my assistance?" Hastings asked. I

couldn't believe how badly I wanted to slap this guy. Or trip him. Or straight-up punch him.

Maybe all three.

Otter's teeth were gritted, his eyes narrowed. "We can't offer you anything else. Thirty percent of the cash is close to nine million dollars. That's nine million dollars that, until we showed up, you didn't have—plus the books we got back for you."

Hastings looked at us for a minute, I think trying to decide if Otter was likely to grab him by the shirt collar again. "Make it thirty-one percent, I'll create the account for you, and I'll give you the dog as a bonus."

"You mean, the dog you're desperate to get rid of? The dog that just ate your bathroom wall?" I said, lifting my eyebrows. "She's not even a purebred, you said it yourself. You're just unloading her on us."

"Right, she's not a purebred—that's why she's not worth anything to *me*. But you guys like her. So make it thirty-one percent, and you can have her *and* my help."

I'll be honest: I expected Otter to scoff. Maybe even to laugh. I didn't expect him to nod, and say, "Fine. Thirty-one percent, and we take the dog now. Ben, go get the man's books from the trunk."

Ben skirted off to retrieve the books while Clatterbuck and I tried not to look too shocked. As Ben and Hastings transferred the books into the case downstairs, I turned to Otter.

"We're *keeping* the dog?" I asked doubtfully.

"For only one percent of the cash. What a bargain," Otter said flatly.

I frowned. "What's your plan?"

"Do I need a plan? Can't I just want a dog?" Otter said.

"You would never just want a dog," Clatterbuck said. "Do you have a fever? Can I check?" He reached forward to put his hand on Otter's head, but Otter slapped it away.

"I'm the director. I said we're keeping the dog," he said.

I wasn't convinced Otter wasn't hiding something from me, but I didn't have time to push it—Ben and Hastings reappeared. Hastings said, "All right, so I'll create the account under your name—Steve, right? You'll transfer the money. I'll get your cash. You'll get the gold. And we'll all be gone before SRS even knows what's happening, right?"

"Exactly. You have the account numbers for the digital money, and the safe deposit box numbers?" Otter asked.

Hastings nodded and handed over a piece of paper with what looked like hamburger grease stains on it. Otter studied it for a moment and then folded it up and slipped it into his pocket. "Well, then. Tuesday. Ten o'clock in the morning, down at the loading dock."

Hastings's mouth twisted up into a weaselly smile. "Perfect."

This was a two-day operation—the longest and most complex thing I'd ever had a part in orchestrating.

Sunday evening, we sat around the kitchen table going over the timetable. Making sure we had everything we needed—the horse trailer. The tour tickets. The boarding passes. The iguana (which wasn't here yet, because we'd have to get that at the last minute). Annabelle circled around us like a furry shark, searching for crumbs we'd dropped at dinner (to be fair, we were so happy to have her back that we all "secretly" fed her under the table).

"All right, day one should be clear enough. A simple smash-and-grab, using Ben's invention and some old-fashioned stakeout time," Otter said. "Day two is where the timing is important. Let's break it down. Beatrix?"

"Uncle Stan and I get to our ride at eight forty-five in the morning," she said.

My turn. "Kennedy, Walter, and I enter the safe deposit room at nine o'clock."

"At nine fifty I hack into the network using the account Hastings created," Beatrix said.

"Nine fifty-five we finish getting the gold loaded and out of the safe deposit room," I said.

"Ten o'clock I make sure everything's been loaded and ready," Walter said.

"At the same time, Hastings moves the cash into the lot at ten o'clock," Otter said. "Supposedly."

"And at ten fifteen I pack everything up and meet you guys to get out of Geneva," I finished.

"Does it bother anyone else that with this plan, there's a good chance Hastings is going to get away with thirty million dollars in cash?" Walter said, frowning.

"The point isn't for us to have the money—it's for SRS *not* to have it," I reminded him, though I actually felt the same way. But hey, Hastings was better than SRS, right?

Which wasn't saying much. But still.

Everyone filtered off to bed—except Walter. He lingered at the table, sort of fidgety, before pulling a thin envelope out from the back elastic of his pajama pants.

"You finished it?" I asked.

"Yeah. But, Hale, I know . . . You don't *have* to do this," Walter said.

"I know. But it'll be fine, Walter. And if it's not safe, I'll just give it back to you, okay?"

"Okay. Thanks, Hale."

"Of course. You'd do it for me, right? Anyway, I've got to go make the call," I said.

"Good luck," Walter said, and grinned as he walked off toward our room. "If this works out, maybe we can recruit her."

I laughed and sat down with the farmhouse's old corded phone and dialed a number Beatrix had hunted down for me. It rang three times, and then a bright female voice answered.

I said, "Is this Aria? Aria Stoneman? Hi, this is—well. My name's Hale, but last time we met, I told you my name was George Kessel. You said I should call you if I was going on a second adventure?"

CHAPTER TWENTY-FOUR

Day One
Mission: Steal the gold
Step 1: Stakeout

Here's what I realized: Being a product of SRS wasn't always a bad thing. It meant that I—and Kennedy, Walter, and Otter—had a pretty good idea of what SRS would do and how they'd do it. SRS was by the books, after all, not an organization known for unique thinking.

Which is why I was staked out with Clatterbuck at a twenty-four-hour pancake restaurant across the street from the bank, wearing a weird blond wig that was supposed to make me look like a random German kid but actually made me look like a random weirdo. I seriously did not have the right skin color for ice-blond hair.

"What if they don't show up?" Clatterbuck asked me under his breath. His fake mustache quivered when he spoke.

"They will—and you don't have to whisper. We're inside. Whispering will only draw attention," I said, then waved to ask the waitress to come refill my juice. I was working hard to make sure she didn't question why a twelve-year-old was in a restaurant at three in the morning—not because I worried she'd throw me out, but because I didn't want her to remember me later. It was safer for her this way, if she didn't realize I was here on a stakeout.

"Is that them?" Clatterbuck asked hurriedly. I used the reflection of a nearby water pitcher to look behind me at the bank. A small truck—they called them LKWs here, and they were basically semitrucks with big flat faces—was pulling up to the bank's service entrance.

"That's them. Everyone, can you hear me? " I asked over the comm. One by one everyone else checked in. "I see them now. They're in an unmarked truck with a blue cab, cleaning company logo on the side. And, Walter? Your mom is definitely with them. I can't see her face, but I recognize her by her walk."

"Great—wait, my mom totally doesn't have a walk!" Walter said.

"She sort of does," Kennedy's voice chimed in on his end. They started to argue, so I tuned them out and focused on the truck and its occupants. The SRS agents spoke with the guard in front of the bank's gates. He scanned a list and then seemed to cross their names off; a moment later he was waving them through. They were there to move their gold. They knew to do it because, as we expected, Hastings had tipped them off about us. In some ways, I hated that Hastings had been so reliably untrustworthy—I wanted him to surprise me and be a decent person. But if he were, our plan wouldn't have even gotten off the ground.

"*L'addition, s'il vous plait,*" I said to the waitress. *Check please.*

Step 2: Route analysis

Clatterbuck and I sped away from the bank in a black pickup truck that belonged to the owners of the *poney* farm. It smelled like horses and was dusty with hay bits, but it was perfect for the mission.

"All right, guys, I've nearly got it—the cameras are slow," Beatrix said over the comm. She was hacking into Geneva's network of traffic cameras, mapping where the truck came from so she could sort out where it would go once they'd loaded up their gold. "It looks like they came from the west, so I'm guessing they'll need to return that way too."

"We'll start working on bodies of water and roads—go get the others," Otter said.

Clatterbuck and I rode in relative silence, save his occasionally whistling, until about ten minutes later. He eased the truck to the side of the road, where Kennedy, Ben, and Walter were waiting alongside an empty horse trailer. Clatterbuck backed the truck up while Walter waved to direct him. By the time Clatterbuck and I got out, Walter was already hooking the trailer up to the truck hitch.

"Finally! Geneva is *cold* at night," Kennedy said, jumping for the truck's open door to get in. She and Walter were both in their black SRS uniforms, which didn't offer much by way of warmth.

"I'm not at all cold," Walter called from the hitch.

Ben scoffed. "Walter ran two miles while we waited."

"One and a half!" Walter corrected, trying to sound offended but mostly looking pleased. He and Clatterbuck climbed back into the truck, and Walter went on. "I have a lot of physical work to do this evening. I can't do it if I'm a Popsicle."

Walter had a point. Plus, if the guy needed to run around to keep from dropping my sister, then I didn't care if he ran ten miles. I turned in the passenger seat to remind Kennedy to stretch out, but she was already in the middle of a split on the truck floorboards. She gave me a *don't worry* look and then pushed her nose down toward her knee so she was in a position that I was pretty sure I could only hit if all my joints were broken.

"Ben, you all set?" I asked.

"Yes. Yes, I'm good," Ben said. He sounded a little frantic, but I wasn't surprised—this was his first time in the field. He opened a red backpack and removed a few gadgets, handing each one to Kennedy. "All right, this is the BENgo—do we need to go over it again?"

"Nope, I'm all set. And the fire is smaller now?" Kennedy asked.

"Yep—good thinking on that. Hale, did you know your sister has a knack for explosives?" Ben said. I grinned at her.

Kennedy beamed. "And I didn't even get to take that class at SRS!"

"And then, Walter, you've got—yes. You've got rope, you've got the pulley, you're all set," Ben said, nodding at the metal pulley in Walter's hands. He smiled at it. "Gotta respect the classics, right?"

Beatrix's voice crackled in over our comms. "Guys? The truck is leaving now. They're taking a weird route, but I think you'll be able to meet up with them on Rue Sous-Terre."

"It's a straightaway?" I asked.

"Of course—sort of like a miniature highway in between villages," Beatrix said, sounding a little offended. I turned over my shoulder to look at Kennedy and Walter, who were gazing at the floor, seemingly rehearsing something in their heads.

Otter's voice broke in. "If I'm right, they should be going over the Rhône River twice—first pass is in thirty minutes, and that's definitely the better choice, if we can get this done by then."

"Copy that," I said. "There they are!"

Ahead of us—way ahead of us—was the truck. Bright-blue flat front, white back with the cleaning company logo. No one would have ever suspected they were moving thirty million dollars of gold. It was clever of SRS to use a truck like this instead of an armored one—armored trucks get robbed frequently, since they so obviously have something valuable inside. Who robs a cleaning company truck? Someone desperate for shiny windows?

Step 3: Line up with SRS's vehicle

"Easy, easy," Clatterbuck said to himself, setting the truck—and the horse trailer—at a nice clip so that we were gaining on the blue truck but not so quickly that they'd be alarmed.

"It's time?" Walter asked me. I nodded; Clatterbuck hit a button to open the sunroof. Before I could even cringe, my sister was climbing out of it, Walter at her heels. They hoisted themselves from the car to the sunroof and then jumped into the back of the truck bed. I didn't really want to watch as Kennedy climbed up the side of the horse trailer, wind whipping at the hair that'd come loose from her ponytail, but I did anyhow, holding my breath the entire time.

"They up?" Clatterbuck asked, his voice calm, his eyes on the road.

"Walter is climbing—yes. They're up. Lying flat now," I said. "Beatrix, you there? We'll need to go dark soon."

"Got it," Beatrix said, though she sounded nervous. "You know it's not 9-1-1 here, right? If she falls? It's 1-1-2."

"Thanks," I said through gritted teeth. The truck was coming up into view. Ben and I ducked down onto the floorboards—well, Ben did. I didn't fit so neatly, but I managed to get down below the windows. "Easy, easy, easy, easy," Clatterbuck chanted. Any change in speed, and they could both topple off the trailer . . .

Step 4: Terrifying and impressive cheerleading tricks

Walter and Kennedy moved so quickly that I almost missed it. She planted her feet in his hands, they bounced one, two, three—and the next thing I knew, my sister was soaring through the space between the trucks, landing neatly on the top of SRS's. Walter then backed up as far as he dared on the trailer; Kennedy braced her knees and held out a hand. Walter ran, leaped—

"They're on, Clatterbuck, back off a little!" I said, cheering a little too loudly. Walter had almost overbalanced on the truck, but Kennedy's arm caught him.

Clatterbuck slowed so that we were just behind the truck, close enough to keep an eye on our agents but far enough back to look like just another driver on a road at night. A few cars zipped along past us, short and neon things, and I was grateful—*if* there was any attention on us, those likely stole it away.

Step 5: Create a door

SRS undoubtedly had an alarm on the truck's back doors—so we weren't going to use them. Instead Clatterbuck, Ben, and I watched as Kennedy knelt and used the BENgo to stamp a circle of dots around her feet, each only a finger-width apart from the others. She and Walter turned their heads away, and suddenly there was a small spark, a little bit of a flame, as the BENgo acids ate through the roof of the truck. Walter kicked the weakened metal circle in and dropped down into the back, out of our sight. Kennedy perched over the hole, watching, her hair eventually coming totally free of its ponytail. Walter was clearing the space, double-checking that there weren't any agents riding with the cargo—

Kennedy gave us a thumbs-up and then dropped down after Walter. I exhaled.

"Are they in? Are they in?" Beatrix asked, and it sounded like she'd been holding her breath.

"We're in—that wind is *serious*," Walter said. "All right, Hale, we're at the container with the gold on it. It's not an electronic combination lock, though; it's biometric."

"What? Biometric?" Otter snapped into the conversation.

"Yep. It's got a mic—voice recognition, I think," Walter said, sounding grim. "Can we still cut into it and disarm it?"

"Let me think," I said.

Otter said, "Not much time to think, Jordan, the river's approaching fast—"

"I know, I know . . . ," I said. The trouble with biometric locks was that there wasn't a *key*. There was just a voice or fingerprint or eye scan, and while you could fake all those things with enough time, it wasn't nearly as simple as picking an old-fashioned tumbler lock or working out the four-digit code of an electronic one.

"Walter? Do you do a good impression of your mother?" I asked.

"Uh, I guess? But you do a better one—"

"Yeah, but you're more likely to have her vocal cord structure. I just pick up her sound when I—never mind. Try your voice on the lock."

"All right," Walter said, but he sounded doubtful.

I heard a few beeps, then a machine said, "Authentication required. Please state your name."

"Teresa Quaddlebaum," Walter said, invoking a little of his mom's trademark glower into the tone.

"Access denied."

Everyone groaned in harmony over the comm.

I said, "You need to get higher, I think."

"I can't get higher!"

"Wait, wait," Beatrix said, typing frantically. "Walter, say your mom's name again to me." Walter did. "Okay, hang on . . . Okay, got it. Hold your comm up to the microphone and try it again."

Walter sighed, but I rustled his comm off. The machine repeated: "Authentication required. Please state your name."

Through the comm, Beatrix played a file—Walter's voice, digitally raised. "Teresa Quaddlebaum."

We waited.

We waited.

And . . .

"Access granted," the voice said, followed by a resounding click.

"You're a genius, Beatrix," I said, shaking my head.

"Oh, I know," she answered. "So now—Kennedy, you should have the pulleys ready?"

"All set," my sister answered.

Kennedy, at this point, was hooking the metal pulley to the top of the truck. She and Walter then got to work, loading gold bars into her owl book bag and hoisting them to the roof, one at a time. Kennedy popped back up onto the roof to offload the bars and stack them neatly, but it was going slower than expected, especially given their weight—she could lift them on her own, but she'd mostly resorted to just sliding them into place. There were fifty-seven bars total—

"How many do you have left?" Otter asked.

"A little over halfway done," Walter grunted; I heard metal clank together as he hoisted another load to the roof. Twenty million in gold, on the top of a truck, zipping along a Swiss road.

"You'll miss the first pass over the Rhône, but you might be able to make the second," Otter said, sounding somewhat frenzied.

"No," I said, "No—Walter, Kennedy, lock the safe back up and get out. We've got most of it, but you're slowing, and the second river pass is only four minutes out. It's not worth the risk."

"Are you sure, Hale?" Kennedy asked.

"Positive. Move," I said, and to my relief, no one questioned me. A good spy sticks to the mission, but a good mission director knows the reality of the situation. SRS would still have ten million, sure, but we'd have twice that, and SRS wouldn't know until the vault reached its final destination, and they opened it up . . .

"Wait! Instead of turning the voice lock back on, reset it. Use Kennedy's voice," I said, nearly shouting into the comm.

"Clever," Clatterbuck said, smirking. SRS would get to keep their ten million, but they'd have quite a time getting through a biometric lock programmed to Kennedy's voice. As Kennedy and Walter scrambled to the roof, Clatterbuck sped up a little so that we'd be close by when Walter and Kennedy had to jump back over. I saw the road curve ahead, and the bridge. This crossing was larger, so Kennedy and Walter would have more time, but it was still a big task . . .

"River approaching," Walter said. "Three hundred feet . . . two hundred . . . one hundred . . ."

"Go!" I shouted.

Walter and Kennedy frantically began to shove the gold bars off the roof—and into the river below. They went one pile at a time, Walter shoving and Kennedy kicking piles over with her feet. A few bars clanked against the guardrails before dropping into the water, but they still made it. Ten million in, fifteen million in, sixteen million, the other side of the bridge and the little village beyond was approaching—

"That's all of them!" Kennedy shouted happily. Ben and I high-fived, and I heard Beatrix celebrating back at the farmhouse. Clatterbuck, however, was even-keeled, getting up closer and closer to the truck. I saw the passenger—it was Mrs. Quaddlebaum—glance at us in her side mirror, but luckily it was too dark for her to notice anything. At least, I hoped it was. Kennedy and Walter walked to the edge of the truck and waited for us to draw closer. I saw Kennedy put her feet in Walter's hands, prep, then soar through the space. She landed squarely on the roof of the horse trailer and then rolled off into the truck bed. Walter was next; he backed up, prepared to run—

The SRS truck hit its brakes.

Not *hard,* but given that Walter was balancing on the rooftop, hard enough. He lost his balance, fell, and rolled down the roof of the truck, but he grabbed ahold of the edge just in time. Clatterbuck had no time to react; he sailed by the SRS truck, and from the floorboards I got a glimpse of Teresa Quaddlebaum glaring into our window, watching our every move, assessing whether the strange horse trailer following them was a threat.

"Keep going, keep going," I hissed at Clatterbuck.

"But, Walter," he said through gritted teeth.

"I'm okay!" Walter panted over the comm. "Go, go, or she'll know something's up!"

Clatterbuck listened, continuing on past the truck without hesitation. We all tensed, waiting to see how SRS would react, because if we were caught, we'd almost certainly know in the next few seconds—if they pulled over to check the gold or the back door locks.

They didn't. They continued along.

"I'm back on the roof," Walter said as we came up on the village. "What should I do, Hale?" I could hear him unraveling—as per usual, Walter didn't react well to a change in plans. We were in a populated part of town—if it were daylight, he'd be able to jump down at a red light, perhaps. As it was the middle of the night, the lights were all green as far as the eye could see.

"Turn here!" I shouted to Clatterbuck.

"But that's a one-way road!" he protested.

"I know!" I argued. Clatterbuck flinched but managed to wheel the horse trailer to the left, between two old brownstone-type buildings. We scratched a few cars parked along its edge, but there was nothing to be done about that—we were in something of a rush. I signaled for Clatterbuck to slow down.

"What are you doing? Where'd you go?" Walter asked shakily.

"We turned down a one-way street—it should signal the traffic lights to change, if they're controlled by a sensor, which they have to be, or there wouldn't be straight greens all down the—yes!" I shouted as the light on the main road flicked to yellow. The SRS truck would have to stop. Clatterbuck turned our truck off so we were hidden by darkness. Behind us, we watched SRS roll to a stop, wait for the light cycle, and then drive on.

Leaving Walter, who looked like he was about three seconds from fainting, at the light.

Ben and Clatterbuck sprinted from the car to retrieve him, whooping in celebration. Kennedy, who'd been flat in the truck bed for most of this, rose up, grinning crazily, her hair a red nightmare from the wind. She watched as Ben and Clatterbuck guided Walter back, causing more than a few irritated apartment dwellers to peer through their curtains at the source of all the yelling.

"We did it?" Kennedy asked, bounding through the back window of the cab like she'd just drunk nineteen sodas. She knew the answer, of course, but she wanted to hear me say it.

I exhaled and pulled the comm out of my ear to give myself a second without the soft static buzz. I smiled— mission control was, in some ways, way more exhausting than actually being in the field. "Well. Once we pull it out of the Rhône, we'll have SRS's gold. And if we've done everything perfectly, they won't have a clue what we've done until after day two."

CHAPTER TWENTY-FIVE

Day Two
Mission: Everything but the gold
(because we already have it—haha, SRS)

In theory, everyone got an hour of sleep between day one and day two of Operation Vengeance for Annabelle. In reality, I think only Annabelle herself slept. I know Walter, Ben, and I tossed around before finally giving up and heading back to the kitchen, where Beatrix was already reading her equipment. She had the earliest call time—at eight forty-five in the morning. She and Otter had to be at the helicopter tour pad.

"Need any help?" I asked her.

"Nope," Beatrix said cheerily. "What about you guys? Want me to double-check the comms before I leave?"

"Nah, they'll be fine," I assured her.

"Take some pictures for me?" Clatterbuck said glumly as he made his way down the hall. He walked up to the espresso machine and prodded at it for a second, and then he grabbed a juice out of the fridge instead. Beatrix promised to take photos, but Clatterbuck still looked a little sad that, while Otter and Beatrix went on the helicopter ride he'd wanted, he, Walter, Ben, and Kennedy would be hiring a boat to retrieve the twenty million in gold we'd dumped into the Rhône.

Unless, of course, SRS realized the gold was missing. In theory, they wouldn't—after all, the back door to the truck hadn't been opened, and the vault was armed. They'd have to be inspecting the roof of the truck to notice anything was amiss, and I suspected the chances were better that they'd merely parked the truck in a facility overnight, with the idea that they'd bring it all back to the bank after they caught us mid-heist.

If we were wrong, I was about to be in a lot of trouble though—because I was the only member of the team who'd actually be *in* the bank. I'd have a comm on to communicate with the others, of course, but no one was running mission control. It was just me this time.

It felt both supercool and superterrifying. I hadn't felt so anxious since I broke into The League headquarters earlier in the summer, looking for my parents, back before I realized who the real good guys were.

Beatrix and Otter left, and after a quick hug, Kennedy bounded off with everyone else, leaving me to take the bus to the bank, which felt extremely un-spylike but gave me some time to settle. To focus. To relax.

Tense spies make mistakes. And at this point, there was no room for mistakes.

I exited the bus and walked across the street, and then I started on the steps to the bank. If I'd gotten my timing right, Hastings should've been arriving at any moment.

There. He was on his way up the steps, wearing a designer suit that had grown too tight on him. He looked clammy, and he fidgeted. He looked *tense*. I gradually made my way toward him so that we wound up at the top of the steps together.

"Mr. Hastings," I said politely as we pushed into the same cubby of the bank's massive revolving door.

"Mr. . . . uh . . . Hale," Hastings said. He looked gleeful, and it was hard to not reach up and smack the grin off his face. In his mind, I was about to get captured by SRS, and he seemed positively *thrilled* about it. Or, I supposed, positively thrilled about the payday my capture would result in. "Where's everyone else?" he asked.

"They're in place—no, don't look! SRS could have someone here. You never can be too careful," I said, making my eyes big and wary.

"Ah, right. Well. I suppose I'll see you at the loading dock, then?" he whispered as we entered the lobby.

"One o'clock," I said, and winked for good measure. Hastings scurried away while I headed toward the main counter. I smiled at the banker there. "I'd like to open a safe deposit box, please," I said in smooth French.

The banker swept me through the process and, after I handed over a fake check, passed me the key to a safe deposit box. I nodded and made my way down to the room, passing through two security officers on the way, each of whom needed to see my key to let me through. The safe deposit vault was, like the rest of the bank, beautiful and ornate. The boxes themselves were copper-gold colored, and the ceiling was painted pale burgundy. There were cameras, one in each corner, and I knew SRS was tapping into them. I wandered around the room, looking at the boxes—casing them, as far as SRS could tell—before finally stopping at box 713. I opened it with my new key, carefully dropped in a small package with holes punched along the top, and then left.

Twelve fifty-three.

"Beatrix, you guys in place?" I asked quietly through the side of my mouth.

"Almost, Hale!" she shouted—she had to shout to be heard over the noise of the helicopter. I was grateful when she muted her comm and the noise of the chopper vanished.

Twelve fifty-five.

Step 1: Simple handoff

I crossed back over to the opposite end of the lobby and sat down on a wood bench, fidgeting and trying to look like I was waiting for a parent to finish some manner of banking business. This bench was one of the few places in the bank that the cameras *didn't* have a great view of— it was in the background of peripheral shots, but nothing was aimed right at it since I was pretty far from the vaults and the bankers.

The revolving doors swung open; in walked three kids wearing black. Or rather, two wearing black, and one wearing dark gray. Aria Stoneman, Jeffery Alabaster, and Archimedes St. Claire (who was the one in a gray T-shirt looking very wary of the entire thing). Aria strode toward me, gave me a passive look, and then sat down on the adjacent bench.

"The jester sleeps in the nest," Archimedes said in a hushed voice.

"Huh?" I asked.

"It's code! Shouldn't you use code or something?" Archimedes said, laughing and elbowing Jeffery.

Jeffery said, "Yeah, you're a spy, aren't you?"

Here was the thing: I told Aria—who told the other two—the truth about everything. Who I was—my first name, anyway. Who SRS was. Who The League was. I even told them why we'd broken into the country club that day. I

didn't do it to be kind of inclusive or awesome or anything. I did it because it was a totally crazy story no one would believe anyway, and yet also was the story most likely to get them to help us.

Except honestly? I think Aria believed me. Which was dangerous but sort of pleasing anyhow.

I slid the safe deposit key across the wooden bench swiftly, almost imperceptibly. Aria caught it with her palm.

"It's box seven thirteen," I said.

Aria slipped the key into her peacoat pocket and tossed her hair over her shoulder. "All right. One oh five. Right? Still one oh five?"

"Exactly," I said.

Jeffery and Archimedes were still shoving each other—they clearly didn't believe this was anything more than a higher stakes golf cart chase. But Aria . . . Aria looked determined. Sort of scared, but determined.

"You don't need to worry. Nothing will happen," I assured her.

She looked at me and grinned. "Nothing? Some adventure this is, Hale. And by the way, next time we talk, remind me to tell you a funny story about the *real* Kessel brothers."

I smiled. "Deal. Well—hoods and hats on, gentlemen," I said to the boys. Their chuckling faded away; Archimedes pulled up the hood of his jacket, and Jeffery pulled out a beanie that said ROWING IS LIFE.

One o'clock.

"Let's go, boys," Aria said smartly, and rose. She walked straight toward the safe deposit boxes, boot heels clacking across the marble floor.

Beatrix's voice appeared in my ear. "They're all set?" she asked.

"Yeah."

"They seem cool. Maybe when we're done, we could all hang out!" she suggested.

"When we're done in Switzerland?"

"No, when we've, like . . . you know. Destroyed SRS and everything. We'll have a lot of free time. We could have a sleepover!" Beatrix said. I wanted to laugh out loud, but I managed to keep my voice down; I heard Otter scoffing through Beatrix's headset.

"He's not invited," I told Beatrix, and she snickered.

Step 2: Get an eye on everything

I rose and walked over to the guard at the front door.

"Excuse me, sir? I'm . . . Well. I'm lost," I said, taking a gulping breath.

"Oh! Oh no!" he said. "Your *maman*! Here, go here, we will her find!" he said with a French accent. He turned and waved his arms at another guard, who was standing at a broad desk, staring at a number of computer screens—the camera feeds. "Go see *mon copain*, Frederick! He will you help!"

I nodded bravely and trotted over to Frederick. The guards radioed about the situation while I was on my way between them; when I arrived at Frederick's desk, he had a piece of chocolate for me and gestured for me to stand just off to his left—where I had a perfect view of the cameras. One oh five—and I could see Aria and her friends in the safe deposit room. I could see Hastings moving the cash from the vault to the loading dock, where an armored car we'd arranged waited. I felt bad for the driver—would he still get paid even though the whole thing was just a ruse?

"Can you describe your mother to me, son?" Frederick the guard interrupted my thoughts kindly.

"Oh, yes. She's tall with dark hair and a straight nose. Her name is Teresa. Teresa Quaddlebaum."

"And your name?"

"Walter Quaddlebaum," I said placidly. "She's here somewhere, I'm sure of it."

I really was. Frederick nodded and turned to his phone to make a few calls, so I focused on the cameras. Everyone was in place, just waiting for the cue.

"Good afternoon, friends of the Central Bank of Switzerland. Will a Mrs. Teresa Quaddlebaum please meet your son, Walter, at the security desk? Thank you." Frederick said—first in English, then in French, then in German.

"That's it—go, Beatrix," I said quietly.

"Yes!" Beatrix cheered. A moment passed, and suddenly I could hear the faint hum of a helicopter outside, hovering over the building, where Beatrix could access the bank's network without actually setting foot inside the bank.

An alarm sounded—small but bright enough to annoy patrons without terrifying them. The guards, however, went wide-eyed and stood up straighter at their stations.

"They know you're in," I muttered.

"Got it, got it, almost there," Beatrix answered, still sounding gleeful. Frederick's walkie-talkie suddenly burst to life; on the cameras I saw men and women in dress shirts pounding away at computers, trying to sort out how someone had cracked their network.

"The roof? How are they on the roof?" Frederick said in response to someone on the walkie-talkie. He spun around to face me. "Stay here, son. We'll get this sorted out. Teresa Quaddlebaum, right?"

"Right."

And Frederick dashed off. I kept an eye on the monitors—

Step 3: Fake League agents fake
rob the safe deposit boxes

Aria and her friends were in the safe deposit room, running their fingers across boxes, looking frantic, just as I'd asked them to. I looked up, saw that it wasn't just the guards running. Five or six adults in street clothing were moving faster than necessary—SRS agents in disguise.

They flew to the safe deposit box vault, looks of glee on their faces, certain they'd caught us in the act.

I watched on the monitor as they burst through the vault door, winced as they grabbed Jeffery's arm and spun him around. There was shouting, shoving, and Jeffery's ROWING IS LIFE beanie fell off. Aria held up her single safe deposit key to prove she belonged there. SRS agents talked into comms, shook their heads, I could read their lips—*It isn't them.* They shrugged over and over.

Then Aria plucked something she'd removed from safe deposit box 713, and the agents jumped back. It was a baby iguana—just like Aria said she wanted back at the country club. The agents went all wide-eyed again, a combination of confused and horrified. Archimedes and Jeffery laughed so loud that I thought I could hear traces of it all the way from the lobby; Aria, meanwhile, cuddled the iguana to her chest. I wondered what she'd name it.

Step 4: Hastings does a lot
of heavy lifting for no reason

I looked back at the camera with Hastings—he had the money into the truck now and was standing impatiently outside the back. The driver was nearby, spinning the keys on his finger, waiting for the go-ahead from Hastings, who was waiting for me or someone else from The League. We were never coming, of course, and unfortunately, SRS would get to keep their cash. It was satisfying, though, to see Hastings panting and sweating from all the money pushing.

"Money is transferring now, Hale," Beatrix said.

"Perfect. Where's it going?" I asked.

"Everywhere. I transferred it to accounts all over the world. Though a considerable amount went to that space camp Ben was talking about—"

Otter cursed in the background.

"And I sent some to a rhino reservation and had them name a baby rhino after you, Agent Otter!" Beatrix said cheerfully.

Otter cursed even louder.

"SRS won't be able to track who got the money?" I asked.

"Nope—Hastings was the one keeping track. And as of right . . . *now*, I've deleted his entire history from the bank. His files, his log-ins, everything. Markus Hastings no longer exists as an employee of the Central Bank of Switzerland, which means his accounts no longer exist."

I looked at Hastings in the camera and then frowned. "Good, because . . . I think he's about to rob them."

"Huh?"

"The armored car guard is lying there unconscious, and Hastings is getting in the driver's seat. He's taking the money!"

"Guess he wants two private islands. Wow. What a jerk—can't he be loyal to *anyone*?" Beatrix said. "Anyway, Otter and I are leaving, Hale. You're good? On your way out the door?"

"Yep." I clicked off my comm.

I'd lied to Beatrix and Otter. There was no way I'd make it to the door—because when I looked up from the monitors, I saw Teresa Quaddlebaum walking toward me. She had a giant artificial smile on her lips and was wearing a navy-blue pant suit that I knew had Kevlar built in. Her hair was nicely curled, and her hands were straining into fists.

"I heard your message!" she said cheerily, but her voice was loaded with poison.

I took a breath. A big one, because Walter's mom scared me even when I was still with SRS.

Step 5: (Confidential) Deliver a message

CHAPTER TWENTY-SIX

"I have something for you," I said seriously.

Mrs. Quaddlebaum dropped the singsong voice a little. "A gift? From The League to SRS? Is it your agents in handcuffs? Because that's what we're after, these days."

"No. It's for *you*. From Walter." I reached into my pocket—Mrs. Quaddlebaum tensed, ready to deflect a weapon—and removed an envelope. "I don't know what it says. I didn't read it."

Mrs. Quaddlebaum looked stunned—this was not part of the mission. This was not something SRS had trained her to deal with. I knew exactly what she was feeling, because the same sensations were running through my gut. Staying at the bank to hand a letter to her was *not* what SRS would instruct me to do. It was *not* an especially wise choice. It was *not* thinking of the mission.

But it was thinking of Walter. So there I was.

"It's just a letter," I said when she didn't take it.

This broke her—she reached forward and snatched it from my hands, and then crammed it into her pocket. "Is it full of lies? Did Walter even write it, Hale? Or is it just more of your brainwashing? Stories about how The League is so fantastic, how your parents aren't traitors, how you didn't *kidnap my son*?" She said all this with an eerie calm to her voice—her training taking over and smashing down the emotions that hid under her easy tone.

"I don't know what it says. I didn't read it," I repeated. "But I know Walter misses you. I miss my parents too, and I would do anything to get a letter to them. So that's why—"

Mrs. Quaddlebaum's head tilted a little. I knew the action—someone was talking in her comm. She kept her eyes on me, but her breathing became heavy and sharp, like a bull's. "What do you *mean* he's gone?" she asked through gritted teeth.

"Oh, you're talking about Hastings. Yeah. He drove off with that armored truck. You didn't pay him already, did you? Because he just robbed you on top of that."

Mrs. Quaddlebaum's hands gripped the desk tightly. She muttered, *"Follow the armored car!"* into her comm, then said to me, "You think you're clever? Because if you think I'm letting your team walk out of this building—"

"My team isn't in this building. I've got two agents in a helicopter robbing your accounts, but right about now everyone else—including Walter—is loading up SRS's gold. So it's just you and me. What can I say, Mrs. Quaddlebaum? SRS taught me well. This was practically an inside job."

Mrs. Quaddlebaum's face grew so tight that it looked like her cheekbones might tear right through her cheeks— they hadn't realized the gold was gone yet. Today was just full of surprises.

I grinned.

Mrs. Quaddlebaum continued, her voice hard and taut, "You've been lucky so far, Jordan, I'll admit that, despite being . . . well"—she gave my body an appraising once-over—"*you,*" she said, spitting the word out. "But fine, then—*you* won't get out of the building. I've got seventeen agents undercover here, ready to take you *out*—"

"I'm standing in the middle of the Central Bank of Switzerland, Mrs. Quaddlebaum, which is one of the most guarded and secured buildings in the country—trust me, I should know, since I was going to rob it," I said shortly. "So, frankly, I'd like to see you and your seventeen agents try."

Teresa Quaddlebaum's eyes lit up. If we were back at SRS, I'd be terrified. No, wait—I was still terrified, actually. She seriously looked like her entire head might explode into flames at any moment. But instead she smiled. "But you're my son, remember? So you'll leave with me, and if you argue, I'll make sure everyone knows how prone you are to tantrums."

"Tantrums? I'm almost thirteen."

"Indeed. I really hope you'll grow out of it," she snapped, and grabbed ahold of my arm. I stumbled along after her. *Think fast, think fast!* I shouted at myself for turning my comm off. I could drop to the floor and shout and scream, but then the police or other SRS agents would get involved. We made it through the revolving doors and to the stairs. I had about as good a chance fighting off Mrs. Quaddlebaum as I did fighting off Walter, which was to say, I had no chance whatsoever. Pigeons flocked overhead, tourists were in the street . . .

An armored car squealed toward the front of the bank.

Which was alarming, but even more alarming was the fact that great, billowy gusts of bright-pink smoke were streaming from the windows, from the back doors, even from the tires. The truck looked like it was bleeding cotton candy. It rammed into one of the traffic barricade pillars; people scattered, shouting in multiple languages, clambering to get away. Mrs. Quaddlebaum and I froze, staring as someone—Hastings!—stumbled from the car, coughing, waving the pink smoke from his face, and coated in liquid of the same color.

"He set off the dye packs," Mrs. Quaddlebaum said. At first I thought she was talking to me, but then I realized she was speaking frantically into her comm. "I don't know! He had to be driving the car, but he somehow set them off. The cash is ruined. I need a pickup—I've got Hale Jordan, at least." She hustled me along as neon-orange-and-white police cars came squealing up, high-pitched sirens screaming. Officers jumped out and knocked Hastings to the ground, and Mrs. Quaddlebaum turned me and pushed me along, but there was no way we could make it off the bank steps without passing the police.

"I see you. We're nearly there," Mrs. Quaddlebaum said to whoever was on the other end of her comm. I followed her gaze—there was a silver car at the corner, idling by a traffic light.

Obviously, I couldn't get in that car.

So I sat down.

This is a thing that, for whatever reason, people never do in movies. You're being taken somewhere? You don't want to go? Drop your weight. Fall to the ground. Because moving someone who is planted on the ground like a sack of potatoes is really, really hard.

Mrs. Quaddlebaum nearly tripped over me and then spun around to stare. "Up, Jordan," she hissed.

"Or what? You'll have a sniper take me out right here? With the cops a few steps away?" I answered. Just as I said that, one of the officers raced by me to assist with the still-pink-smoking car, knocking Mrs. Quaddlebaum in the shoulder. She glowered. It seemed entirely possible that pink smoke might come out of *her* ears.

Mrs. Quaddlebaum looked around—police tape was going up now, and we were some of the only "civilians" still on the steps. She stooped and wrapped her arms around my shoulders and heaved. She couldn't lift me. She tried another angle, then another angle . . .

"I'm going. He won't move, and I can't lift him. This kid weighs as much as a full-grown man, remember? I need backup," she snapped into her comm. "We can't just leave him! He stole from us! He ruined the Castlebury outpost! He brainwashed my son!"

Then Mrs. Quaddlebaum went silent, and I knew what her mission director was telling her. *Think of the mission.*

I felt bad for her for a second. Not even because I could tell she missed Walter, even if she was being a jerk about it. I felt bad for her because her mission had fallen apart. They'd been robbed, and they hadn't managed to capture a single League agent, much less all of us. We'd duped them again. It wasn't so much that she'd be *punished* for a failed mission. It was that she'd punish herself for not being good enough, strong enough, smart enough. Not being *SRS* enough.

I'd been there.

Of course, I only felt bad for her for that *second*, because I still had to escape. I reached up as discreetly as I could and clicked my earpiece back on.

"Hale? *Hale?*" Beatrix was shouting into the comm.

"I need a way out," I muttered into the comm. Mrs. Quaddlebaum was still listening intently to her own comm and looking at the police, pink smoke, and news chopper–filled skies surrounding us.

"I'm going to *kill you*. You can't just disappear for twenty minutes like that! Everyone's freaking out!" Beatrix yelled. "But Otter is almost there. He's in the black truck from the farm. He won't be able to drive past the police barricades though—"

"I'll handle it. Hale, be ready to run," Otter broke in, and despite the static over his comm, he sounded . . . well. He sounded pretty impressive, actually. He had steel in his voice that made me feel pretty good about whatever he had planned. Mrs. Quaddlebaum wheeled back around to look at me and then dropped down low so no one could hear what she said next.

"Hale Jordan, I'm going to make this very, very clear. You may have been my son's best friend once, but I will not hesitate to use the *full extent* of my training . . ." She kept talking, but I was using my peripheral vision to watch for the black truck sliding up behind the police cars, just barely visible behind the smoke. I saw a flash of my sister's red hair, movement . . . Something was happening . . .

"You understand, Jordan? So get. Up. Right. Now," Mrs. Quaddlebaum hissed. She *also* sounded pretty impressive, but in that totally frightening way. Watching the truck as best I could, I rose. Mrs. Quaddlebaum looked pleased with the effectiveness of her threats and squeezed my arm, prodding me along in front of her.

I dragged my feet, stalling as best I could. I said, "You've got one thing wrong, Mrs. Quaddlebaum. I wasn't your son's best friend *once*—I'm his best friend *now*. And so that's why, despite the fact that you're still with the bad guys, I'm not going to turn you away when you eventually come to The League, asking to join us. Asking for safety. Asking for our help."

More movement from the truck. We were getting closer to it, but now we were just as close to it as we were to SRS's silver car. Otter needed to hurry.

Otter, you're a genius, I thought, grinning as I realized what Otter's plan was. I kept talking, louder now, and turned around to look at Mrs. Quaddlebaum—but more important, to get her looking right at *me* instead of what was happening behind me. I said, "I'll even introduce you to everyone there. The twins. Agent Clatterbuck. You already know most everyone, of course—my sister, Agent Otter, and of course, Walter. And of course, you already know Annabelle."

Mrs. Quaddlebaum frowned. "Who?"

I ducked.

And Annabelle, who had charged through the police barricade, tongue flying, ears flapping, drool drooling, soared into the air. She was leaping for *me*, of course, but when I ducked, all sixty-eight kilos of not-really-purebred Tibetan mastiff slammed into Mrs. Quaddlebaum.

For the second time in five minutes, I felt bad for her. I'd been there too—"there" meaning on the ground with a Tibetan mastiff sitting on me.

"Go, Jordan!" Otter roared in my ear.

"Annabelle, come on!" I called. Annabelle, who looked incredibly confused about how she'd aimed for a stocky boy yet ended up on top of a lanky lady, jumped off Mrs. Quaddlebaum, pawing her right in the kidneys. We charged away as Mrs. Quaddlebaum wobbled to her feet, stumbling forward and grabbing the nearest police barricade for balance. I was slow, but I moved faster than she did at that moment—by the time she waved frantically to the agents in the silver car, I was already diving into the open door of the truck. I had enough sense to roll to the side so Annabelle didn't jump in right onto me, and Otter slammed on the gas, squealing away before the police—or SRS—even had time to process what had just happened.

"I've got him," Otter told the others, glancing at me in the rearview mirror as I grabbed Annabelle's head and rubbed her ears. She looked delighted with herself—I think she knew that this time, tackling someone was a good thing.

"Right, boss man," Clatterbuck said over the comm. "Setting up the plane now. We're ready to leave when you are."

"Is *that* why you let us take Annabelle? Did you know this would happen? This was your plan?" I asked Otter.

"Don't be thick, Jordan. Of course not. Can't I just like a dog?" Otter growled at me, shaking his head.

I opened my mouth in either surprise or to argue (I hadn't decided which), but Beatrix cut me off. "Hale—are you still on your comm? Hale?" I confirmed I was, and she went on, "How did you trip the dye packs? What'd you build the transmitter out of? Or was it some button at that bank guard station?"

"Huh? I didn't trip them. Hastings did."

"Dye packs either get tripped by a radio signal or because someone handles them. He couldn't have handled them since he was driving, so it had to be a radio signal. In fact, I can actually find the radio signal . . . Hang on. Yep. Right here."

"I didn't do that. Seriously. I figured Hastings was just going to get away with the cash," I said, finally clambering to the front seat and buckling in.

"Hold on. I'll trace it," Beatrix said.

Clatterbuck swerved to avoid yet more police cars. I noticed a few news helicopters buzzing overhead. I guess it's not every day that a bank gets robbed, much less that it gets robbed and the culprit winds up stumbling around in neon pink. I *almost* felt bad for Hastings. He'd helped us rob SRS, after all. But then, he'd also meant to sell us out, and then he robbed the bank himself, and he was also kind of a crummy person in general, so . . .

"There's a Morse code layered into the dye pack signal. Hang on. I'm translating," Beatrix said. She mumbled letters, pulling them together to form words. Then she went silent.

"What? What is it?" I asked.

"It says . . . 'Happy Early Thirteenth Birthday, Hale. Love, Mom and Dad.'"

CHAPTER TWENTY-SEVEN

So, here's something that's difficult: getting more than a ton of gold bars out of a country without raising a few red flags. Which meant that all the gold we stole from SRS and scuba-dived out of the river? We left it in Switzerland in a new account we created at a *different* bank—Archimedes St. Claire's father's bank, as a matter of fact. In the end, we took only seven bars back to the United States—one hidden in each of our luggage— with one extra bar used to pay for the plane we took home. Clatterbuck flew, though Otter offered a lot of commentary on his piloting skills and Ben kept pulling panels off walls to look at plane-wiring schematics, making everyone nervous.

"Finally," Beatrix said as she threw open the back door to League headquarters and inhaled deeply. "Oh, wow, it *still* smells like corn chips!" She didn't sound sad about this at all.

"Trust me, that's never going away," Clatterbuck answered.

"We're home, Annabelle! Are you excited?" Kennedy asked the dog. Annabelle responded by bounding among all our rooms, working out the shortest route between each. Otter went off to make spreadsheets or something, and Clatterbuck hurried around, turning things like the air-conditioning and water back on. Ben and Beatrix went back and forth between the car and the building, carefully unloading computer and inventing equipment.

"Want help?" Walter asked as I struggled with my gold-bar-containing suitcase on the steps. I nodded, and Walter slung the suitcase over his shoulder. Then he navigated both mine and his up to the hall where our bedrooms were. He slid mine into my room and then nodded curtly and started toward his own.

"Walter. Don't you want to know?" I called after him. My voice bounced down the long hall. Walter turned around.

"What?"

"If she took the envelope. If she said anything. If she did anything?"

Walter spun his suitcase around under his palm for a second and then shook his head. "No. Well, I do, but only if it's good. If she was . . . If she was all SRS agent-y then . . . no. I'd rather not."

"She took the envelope," I told him, and he nodded.

"Well. It's a start. Maybe she'll . . ." Walter sighed heavily and looked down. "I can't believe after everything, SRS still has a hold on her."

"They had a hold on all of us once. But we chose to leave, so they don't *really* own us—it just feels that way. Your mom will break out eventually. And when she does, she has to take a room down at the end of the hall where Otter stays, because otherwise you'd always be grounded."

"For what?" Walter asked, grinning.

"Well, the music, for one. But also those bikini girl posters."

Walter blanched. "Oh, wow. I'd have to get rid of those."

"Yep."

"Speaking of, I got you something for your birthday. It's not a secret message encoded in a dye pack release signal or anything, but it's something," Walter said, then motioned for me to follow him to his room. Once inside, Walter flung his suitcase on the bed and then opened it; he tried and failed to quickly move the stuffed frog from the suitcase and tuck it underneath the blankets. When he looked back to see if I'd noticed, I pretended like I'd just been looking at some origami cranes folded on top of his dresser.

Walter reached to the bottom of the suitcase, where he had something folded up tightly. He pulled it out and handed it to me. I lifted an eyebrow, took it, and carefully unfolded it. It was a world map—a giant one, bigger than I was. There were dots all over it—most in yellow, and a few in bright green.

"What are these?" I asked.

"The green ones are where you've been on missions," Walter said, pointing—most of the dots were around League headquarters, but then there was one in Geneva and one in Somerset by Wookey Hole. "And the yellow ones are where your parents have been on missions. Recently, anyway. Kennedy had to help. I thought it might be cool, though, to see where you've been that your parents have been? Maybe see where they go a lot? So you can . . . you know. Know you've all been in the same places. That sort of thing."

I stared.

"It's . . . Sorry. It's dumb. It's all I could afford. Well, it was, anyway. I guess technically I now have a half-million-dollar gold bar—"

"It's awesome, Walter. Thanks," I said, still staring, because it was basically the perfect birthday present, but I didn't want to get all sappy with Walter. Now I didn't know what to say, except, "Thanks. Again. It's . . . It's really awesome."

Walter looked pleased. "I'm glad you like it. Especially because I'm pretty sure Otter got you coupons."

"Wow. *Otter* got me a birthday present?"

"Coupons, Hale. He got you coupons. Did you hear that part?"

"Still," I said, and grinned as I left the room. Once I was back in my own, I hung the map up over my bed. It took up the entire wall, and I had to steal a whole bunch of push pins from the bulletin board to make it stay. It made the entire room look brighter, what with the blue oceans and bright pastel countries. I sat at my desk and stared at it for a long time.

Where were my parents now? Surely, not Geneva, not anymore. Maybe not even Europe. I let my eyes wander across countries and continents, waiting to feel some sort of pull, some sort of click that told me I was looking in the right spot. Except, it didn't come. I didn't know where they were.

But they knew where I was. They were watching. They were there, even if I didn't notice, even if there were no messages in the paper, even if birthdays were now accompanied by bank heists and dye packs. It was *dangerous* for them to stick so close to me. It was dangerous of them to send a message to me on my birthday. They'd done it anyway.

Because they didn't *always* think of the mission. They were former SRS agents, after all, but they were also just Mom and Dad.

Everyone at The League threw me a surprise party when my actual birthday rolled around a week later.

Only, it wasn't really even close to a surprise because, for a group of elite spies, they were really terrible at keeping it a secret. Still, there was cake and ice cream, and Clatterbuck bought a piñata that I was terrible at hitting, but Walter pummeled it so well, I felt bad for the piñata. Beatrix and Ben rigged some fireworks to go off the roof in celebration (and by fireworks, I mean explosives that Ben mixed together), so that night we all gathered on the roof and watched them spiral into the sky.

My parents weren't there, but all in all, it was a pretty excellent birthday. Plus, since we were at The League rather than at SRS, I could eat the cake again for breakfast the next morning. SRS would never have allowed that.

"So, what's on the list?" I asked Otter as we sat in the cafeteria post-fireworks show. Kennedy, Walter, and the twins were playing with Annabelle among the remains of the piñata, and Clatterbuck was dozing off in the corner, legs splayed out like a dropped marionette. Otter gave me a questioning look instead of answering my question, so I clarified. "The money. What's on the list of stuff we're doing with the money?"

"You're not the director, Jordan. You don't need to know—"

"You got me coupons for my birthday," I reminded him.

"Those are good—"

"Three of them are already expired."

Otter rolled his eyes, but at least he looked a little embarrassed. "Fine. One million goes to repairs on the building—apparently we need a new roof. One million goes to getting a few essentials—better security, mostly, since now that we've robbed SRS we might want to put some laser wires around the doors. And the rest . . . well. The rest we'll use. Travel, mostly. We'll need it, with the missions I've got planned."

"What missions?"

"Hale, it's your thirteenth birthday. Go take another whack at that piñata Walter killed. Eat some more cake. Stop being a spy for a minute."

I rolled my eyes at him, but I got up anyway and joined everyone near the piñata carcass. Annabelle was there too, snuffling around on the floor for stray pieces of candy.

"Show Hale!" Ben shouted to Kennedy.

"Okay, okay. I taught Annabelle a trick. Plan B, remember? Training her to make money on her own?" Kennedy asked.

"You trained *this dog* to do something useful?" I asked in disbelief.

"Yes! Watch." She grabbed a paper plate and then quietly walked across the cafeteria till she was on the complete opposite side, near the buffet lines (that hadn't actually held food in years and years). She reached into her jacket pocket and removed a little can of dog food, which she popped open and dumped onto the plate. She sat it down, then—

"Annabelle! Dinner!" she called.

Annabelle, who'd been sleepily gnawing on the piñata's dismembered ear, leaped to her feet and ran—I mean *ran*—to the plate of food, smacking at it like it was a gourmet meal. It was gone in seconds.

"You trained her . . . to eat?" I asked as Kennedy walked back, grinning. Everyone applauded.

"To eat beautifully, every time, like she *loves* it," Kennedy corrected me. "I posted a video of it online and two dog food companies are interested in her for commercials. They pay four hundred dollars per commercial, and free food for two months!"

"Four hundred dollars. Whatever did we steal the gold for?" Otter asked drily, but his eyes betrayed him—he was impressed. "All right, everyone—if we're done with the birthday thing, we should head to bed. We've got to be on the mission control deck at zero eight hundred hours."

"For what?" Beatrix asked.

Otter was already walking away, but he responded over his shoulder, "For another mission. What'd you expect? You're spies, aren't you?"